HARD WATER BLUES

HARD WATER BLUES

ROBERT WANGARD

Robert Wangard (signature)

AMP&RSAND, INC.

Chicago • New Orleans

ISBN 978-145070624-7

Design
David Robson, Robson Design

Cover photographs
Walk Softly Photos

Published by
Ampersand, Inc.
1050 North State Street
Chicago, Illinois 60610

203 Finland Place
New Orleans, Louisiana 70131

In Memory of Ed Hoch

PREFACE

When Edward D. Hoch died in January 2008, the world lost one of its foremost authors of short crime fiction. By most accounts, he wrote over 950 stories during his illustrious career. His work was a regular feature in *Ellery Queen Mystery Magazine* (*EQMM*), the gold standard in his field. Incredibly, since 1973, when he made his first sale to *EQMM*, he had a story in every issue of that magazine.

He was also a giant of the mystery community in other ways. Not only was he the past president and a Grand Master of Mystery Writers of America, but he won numerous awards in his field. He counted an Edgar and two Anthony awards among his honors. He also edited an annual anthology of the best mystery short fiction for many years.

In an era when crime-fiction is replete with stories of serial murderers and other gory fare, Ed's stories were notable for the charm and innate goodness of his characters. There'll never be another like him.

While my output is only a speck on Ed Hoch's resume, this collection is dedicated to his memory. The stories in

Hard Water Blues that have been previously published have been revised, sometimes significantly, for purposes of this anthology. Pete Thorsen, the protagonist of *Target*, my first novel, made his initial appearance in one of the stories, "The Last Deal." More importantly, the collection contains a host of completely new material. For example, Pete continues to hold center stage in stories like "Fats Is Dead," which chronicles a weekend reunion with an old army buddy who makes a stunning confession at frozen Crystal Lake; and "Leif Erikson's Ghost," in which the famed Viking's calling card shows up in a very mysterious way. For Pete Thorsen fans, there are other stories as well to satisfy their appetites.

Among other stories, a lonely man yearning for a little excitement in his life discovers, in "The Night They Closed Baker's Bar," the chilling truth that timing is everything. And "The Novelty of Deceit" explores the extent to which a man will go to protect his ill-gotten gains.

Finally, my second novel, *Malice*, another Pete Thorsen mystery, is due out in 2012. You can read the first chapter at the end of this book.

Enjoy!

Robert Wangard
Hinsdale, IL

CONTENTS

STORIES

MALICE

STORIES

FATS IS DEAD

ete Thorsen was having second thoughts. Talking with his old army buddy on the telephone for a half-hour was one thing; spending a weekend with him was another. He wasn't sure he'd even recognize him after all these years.

The latter concern was put to rest when he saw the six-four Jimmy Ray Evans emerge from the crowd at the airport. He wore a fringed leather jacket and a Western-style felt hat that looked like it had been purchased just for the occasion. Some clothes on wire hangers, protected only by a dry cleaner's thin plastic sheath, were slung over one shoulder and his free hand clutched a worn shopping bag. Pete smiled. You could take the boy out of West Virginia, but....

"Hey, partner!" Jimmy Ray cried in a booming voice when he saw Pete wave a hand to attract his attention.

He pushed through the crowd and dropped everything in a pile in his haste to reach his old friend. Then he wrapped his arms around Pete and gave him a long bear hug. When he finally released him, he held him at arm's length and beamed.

"Look at you!" he exclaimed. "Ain't changed a bit since our soldiering days!"

Pete wasn't much for public displays of affection, and stood there with Jimmy Ray's hands on his shoulders and a lopsided grin on his face. He mumbled, somewhat self-consciously, "Maybe a little fatter and grayer."

"Oh, bullshit! I got a good memory, and you could still be a young buck private in the old 2nd Cav!"

In spite of his reservations, Pete had to admit that it was good to see Jimmy Ray again. He'd been sitting in his office one blustery February afternoon, thinking about his life, when the phone rang. It was Jimmy Ray. It took Pete a minute to put everything in context, which wasn't surprising since it had been 30 years since he'd seen or even talked to him. With Jimmy Ray, though, it didn't take long to get the conversation rolling. After a few minutes of pleasantries, he was yapping away about the old days like they'd just seen each other last week. He reminisced about people in their unit and laughed and told war stories.

Before Pete knew it, Jimmy Ray had invited himself to Chicago for the weekend to get reacquainted. When Pete protested that he already had plans to go up to his cottage on Crystal Lake, Jimmy Ray shifted gears as smoothly as a skilled driver approaching a hairpin turn in his new Porsche and allowed that wouldn't be a problem. He'd always wanted to see the "north country" anyway, he said. Pete ran up the white flag under Jimmy Ray's blitzkrieg of words and agreed to pick him up at the Traverse City Airport.

"You got any food in this town?" Jimmy Ray asked pointedly. "Man, I could eat a moose! This is moose country, ain't it?"

Pete explained that northern Michigan was the domain of whitetail deer, then made a detour downtown and talked their way into the always-crowded Amical for lunch. Jimmy Ray polished off two omelettes with every filling the restaurant had to offer, a basket of bread, and some gooey desert. It was easy to see why he'd put on 25 pounds over the years, although the weight was well-distributed on his tall frame and he didn't look particularly fat. Chunkier, maybe, but not fat.

After giving Jimmy Ray a tour of the Traverse City area, they headed for Crystal Lake. The traffic on the two-lane highway was light, and as they motored west, Pete glanced over at his passenger. He was staring out the side window like a little boy approaching Disney World.

"How did you find my number?" Pete asked. Jimmy Ray glanced his way with a blank look in his eyes, then turned back to the window again without speaking. He seemed to find the stand of jack pines they were passing fascinating. "Look at those trees, will you," he said in a quiet voice. "Trunks as straight as arrows."

Pete thought it strange that Jimmy Ray hadn't responded to his question. He seemed to have heard it. The timber along the highway gradually became a little more diverse as they motored on. Jimmy Ray continued to stare. "God, I love those birches," he muttered in the same low voice.

"Beautiful trees," Pete agreed this time.

Jimmy Ray looked over at Pete with that distracted look again. "I had a wall calendar a few years ago with all these birches along a lake," he continued. "It was a place in Finland, I think. I promised myself I'd go there sometime and see those birches."

Pete nodded. "You should," he said.

When they got to Crystal Lake, Jimmy Ray was looking out the passenger-side window again like he was mesmerized. "I'll be damned," he muttered softly, as if speaking to himself again. "Look at those birches. I wonder if this was the lake on that calendar."

The lake was finally frozen over after a warm start to the winter and the sun was gauzy and low in the mid-afternoon sky. Fishing shacks dotted the ice. A brisk wind kicked up swirls of snow that gave the ice sculptures along the beach an eerie look.

Inside the cottage, Pete busied himself getting a fire started while Jimmy Ray poked around.

"What's this stuff?" Jimmy Ray called, holding up a bottle.

Pete glanced his way. "Thor's Hammer," he answered. "It's vodka."

"Never heard of it."

Pete grinned. "You know who Thor was, though, right?"

"No, should I?"

"Thor was the old Norse god of thunder and lightning. He gave his name to the best vodka around."

"Let me guess — this stuff is made in Norway, right?"

"Actually, Sweden, but it's still good."

Jimmy Ray looked at his watch. "I'd have a martini, but it's only four-thirty."

"It's six somewhere. There's vermouth on the top shelf. Help yourself. I don't have any olives or lemons, though."

Jimmy Ray snorted. "They just mess up a good drink, anyway." He mixed a martini and carried it to the window where he studied the lake intently. "What are those little houses on the ice?" he asked.

Pete finished with the fire, poured himself a glass of pinot grigio, and replied, "Fishing shacks."

"Fishing shacks!" Jimmy Ray exclaimed, shaking his head. The martini must have cleared his head, because he seemed back to his old self. "Shit, where I live, the only thing cold when we go fishing is a six-pack of Jax. Temperature below 80 degrees and we all complain about the cold snap."

"You've got to be tough to be a fisherman up here," Pete said, grinning.

"Tough, hell. We got another name for it."

This time Pete laughed. That was the Jimmy Ray he remembered. Wisecracks coming like bursts from an old-time Gatling gun. He thought again about his army buddy's momentary distraction in the car, and shifted to memories of how his late wife, Doris, loved Crystal Lake. They'd often talked about coming up at this time of year, but somehow had never gotten around to it. It would have been fun to walk out on the ice and go cross-country skiing on the golf course and afterward enjoy a glass of wine in front of the fireplace. Instead, here he was reminiscing with an old army buddy.

Jimmy Ray was busy peering through Pete's telescope. "What's that hole in the ice?" he asked.

"Let me see." Pete refocused the telescope and looked through the lens. "I think that's where they cut out ice to make a sculpture."

Jimmy Ray's face was sober and dark. "Looks like a grave," he said solemnly.

Pete squinted through the telescope again. "It does kind of look like a grave," he said.

Jimmy Ray's eyes looked glassy. "They ever have any people go missing up here in the winter time?" he asked.

From the expression on his face, Pete concluded he was serious. "I don't know. I've never been up here in the winter."

"I tell you, that's a grave," Jimmy Ray persisted, looking through the telescope again. "Look at the size. A man could fit in there easy." He stared at the hole in the ice some more. "What would happen to a person if he got dumped through a hole in the ice like that?"

"I don't know," Pete replied, thinking the conversation had gotten a little weird again. He remembered talking to a friend the summer before when Cara Lane's body was found in the lake. In cold water, his friend had told him, a body stays down for a long time. Warm water is the thing that causes gases to form and for the body to become a floater. He shrugged and said, "I suppose the body would stay down until the ice melted and the water warmed up."

"Umm," Jimmy Ray mused. "I wonder if there's a body down there."

Jimmy Ray eventually lost interest in the hole in the ice, and he began to rummage through Pete's CD collection. He slipped a Roy Orbison disc into the player and went into his DJ routine, using a Coke bottle as a mic. "Here's the great Roy Orbison, folks. Nice and easy now." The lyrics filled the room, and during an instrumental interlude, he interjected, "It sure is cold up here at Crystal Lake, folks. I'm looking at a whole lot of hard water."

Pete smiled at the comment. "Hard water?"

"You know, ice. Hard water. Get it?"

Pete shook his head and continued to smile. "When people say hard water around here, they usually mean water with a high mineral content. Iron and stuff like that."

"That's the trouble with you Yankees. Down South, our language is so much more descriptive. We give names to things we can see. And I sure do see a heap of ice out there."

"I've missed your keen insights, Jimmy Ray."

Jimmy Ray grabbed the telescope again and appeared to be looking at the far end of the lake. "What are those buildings way down there?" he asked, pointing. "More fishing houses?"

Jimmy Ray always had eyes like a hawk, which made him the number one marksman in their unit. "That's the town of Beulah," Pete replied, knowing what he was looking at without checking it out. "The town was built mainly on the old lakebed exposed when some entrepreneur drained half the water out back in the nineteenth century. He wanted to create a navigable channel out to Lake Michigan." Pete told Jimmy Ray the story which had become part of the local lore. He waited for a comment by Jimmy Ray and wasn't disappointed.

"That's you northerners again. You call him an entrepreneur; we call him a damn fool."

Pete chuckled again. "A lot of people up here called him a fool, too." They stared at the "hard water" some more and then Pete turned to Jimmy Ray and asked, "I guess you didn't hear me in the car, but I'm surprised you were able to track me down after all these years."

"No problem," Jimmy Ray replied like he was hearing the question for the first time. "You remember our old outfit? I don't know if you're aware of it, but in 1992, they closed Merrell Barracks where we were stationed. Since then, all these websites have sprung up with lists of guys who served in the 2nd Cav. Your name appeared on a lot of the lists and the 'where are they now' information on some of them said you were a lawyer in Chicago. A couple even gave the name of your firm. From there, it was a piece of cake to get your phone number. You seemed to draw a blank when I called, though. I was kinda hurt."

"It has been a long time, Jimmy Ray," Pete said defensively.

"That it has, my friend, that it has."

Pete stared at the frozen lake again. "You said a lot of sites have been created on the web, huh?" He shook his head. "Who has time to sit around and do stuff like that?"

"You forget, Pete, that for a lot of guys, those days were the highlight of their lives. I remember once about 10 years ago being asked to provide music for a reunion of some guys from one of the units in our division. Not our company — another unit. God, the stories some of those guys would tell."

Pete thought back. Merrell Barracks in Nürnberg, Germany had a storied history. During the war, it had been the barracks for Nazi SS troops and was still known to many of the locals as the SS Kaserne. He remembered all of the underground escape tunnels and the Nazi artifacts — weapons, bayonets, helmets, grenades — they'd found down there. Most of the items had been housed in a small museum on post.

"To listen to guys at that party," Jimmy Ray said, "you'd think they were still fighting the Nazis when we were there and discovering all that stuff in the museum. It was a lot of fun listening to them, I can tell you that."

"I bet."

Jimmy Ray got a nostalgic expression on his face again. "Remember how it was when we were in town drinking beer and missed the curfew? If you knew the ropes, all you had to do was tell the taxi driver about the hole in the fence on the back side of the Kaserne. If your driver didn't speak English, you just guided him back there with sign language. Hell, the drivers who'd been around a while took you straight back to the hole without even being asked."

"Getting back on base wasn't a problem for me," Pete said.

"Sure, it wasn't a problem for you, but most guys didn't carry their passes around in their pockets like you did."

Pete reflected on those days and how he'd lucked out with his assignment. He'd been an ordinary slug, polishing canons and biding his time until duty hours were over and he could hit the bar on post or go into town. Then one day his company commander announced that a major in the CID needed a temporary driver and asked for volunteers. His hand shot up along with a dozen others. The captain, who happened to be looking his way at the time, pointed at him and said, "Okay, Thorsen, you're it, but if I hear one word about you messing up, your ass is alfalfa and I've got the mower."

That marked the beginning of a beautiful relationship that lasted through the end of his tour of duty in Germany. Pete and the major hit it off from the beginning, and while the assignment remained "temporary," it continued for the duration. He kept his pass in his pocket just in case the major should need him at some odd hour. He even got to participate in an investigation on occasion, the most sensational one involving a sergeant from another unit who was found naked, and very dead, near one of the gates to the old city. He'd sometimes wondered whether the excitement of those days accounted for the dogged way he pursued his belief that Cara Lane had been murdered instead of innocently drowning as most people seemed to believe.

Jimmy Ray looked pensive. "You know, I always thought you'd go to Officer's Candidate School and be a lifer."

Pete's brows inched up his forehead. "I don't know where you got that idea. I just used the army to escape from the North Woods. It was pure luck that I landed a cushy job that let me carry my pass 24/7."

"Those were fun days, though," Jimmy Ray said, shaking his head. "Drinking beer at the volksfests. Man, we put away some suds, didn't we?"

Pete grinned. "I remember one time we were sitting with that German family at a fest and you tried to move in on the daughter. The old man kept you away from her like a cowboy on a cutting horse."

Jimmy Ray's face lit up like a neon sign on a cheap motel. "I remember that. She was something. I got up from the table and went to take a piss and came back and slid in beside her. I thought I had it made. After a few minutes, I moved my leg over so it was against hers. She pressed back. Kind of a sign, you know? Then that fat shit of a father, who hadn't peed all day, gets up and goes in search of the latrine. He comes back in about two minutes — I don't think he even relieved himself — and wedges his double-wide ass right between me and the chick. All that maneuvering right down the drain."

Pete grinned again. "He smelled a wolf. Dickie Aug fared pretty well, though, as I recall." Dickie Aug was the third soldier assigned to their squad room. Aug was an affable farm boy from Minnesota and harbored the same itch as Jimmy Ray, only was less obvious about it.

Jimmy Ray shook his head. "Dickie Aug. He was the biggest wolf of all. Face like a friggin' choir boy, but pure wolf. You know what that sonofabitch did? He sucked up to the old man that day and got himself invited to their house for dinner. Weiner schnitzel, that funny little pasta, the whole works.

Then he takes the daughter for a walk by the Dutzendeich and drills her. You remember the Dutzendeich — that lake near where Hitler used to hold his rallies? Dickie had a favorite place down near the water where he took all his girls. You know what his shtick was? He told them he was learning to speak German. He got them to teach him a few words, and then, wham! He was humping before they even knew it. Shit, I could speak more German than he even dreamed of, but as we all know, he looked like a damned choir boy. He got more women than all of us put together."

"You should have invited Dickie," Pete said. "We could have had a 203 reunion."

"Two-o-three?"

"You know, our squad room."

"Oh, sure." Jimmy Ray got a faraway look in his eyes. After a few moments he said, "You know, I tried. I found Dickie on the Internet and sent him four emails. No answer. I tried to call, too, but he's got an unlisted number or some bullshit. You, your number popped right up, but old Dickie — zippo. Probably happily married and doesn't want contact from his old buddies."

"Speaking of marriage, I take it you're not married, Jimmy Ray?"

"Not now," he said wistfully

When he didn't volunteer any details, Pete asked, "But you were at one time?"

"Shit, try four times."

Pete knew that Jimmy Ray liked women, but four marriages? Pete tried to act like four was the nationwide standard, then asked casually, "What happened?"

"You mean to my marriages? Oh, different things." The window looking over the lake had begun to frost up and he walked over and tried to wipe it clean with a sleeve. "Too much of an appetite, I guess. You remember I was born in West Virginia. My Daddy was a coal miner. He gave me some advice when he thought I was going to follow him down in the mines. He said, 'When you're down below and wondering if you'll ever see light again, I don't want you thinking about what it would be like to bang Susie or Lorraine or Marilou. Take them while you can still breathe. Live life like every day's the last time you'll see light.' I guess I took his words a little too much to heart."

Pete murmured, but didn't comment. He'd met a lot of men like Jimmy Ray, but didn't really understand them. Doris was the only woman he ever wanted.

"How about Dickie?" Jimmy Ray asked. "You think he ever screws around anymore?"

"No idea."

"I bet he does. A man don't change his fur when he's got the itch like Dickie."

Pete just shrugged.

Pete rose from his chair, stretched and looked out the window again. The fishing shacks were deserted and the hole in the ice looked forbidding in the fading light. Still, he was struck again by the peacefulness of it all. Not like the hustle and bustle of July and August when everyone was at the lake trying to pack in as much recreation as possible.

Jimmy Ray was flipping through Pete's CD collection again. "I must have trained you pretty good. You have a lot of good music here."

"I learned at the knee of the master," Pete replied. Jimmy Ray was the one who'd put him onto oldies. He was convinced that only music produced before 1980 — with a few exceptions — was worth listening to. Consequently, Pete's collection consisted largely of oldies and classical music. Friends like Harry McTigue never seemed to tire of razzing him about his taste in music, often accusing him of buying it from late-night infomercials for $29.95 a pop. That made Pete laugh; he tried never to pay more than half that amount for any CD.

In their army days, Jimmy Ray's dream was to become a famous disc jockey specializing in the "real" music. He played his favorites over and over and was gaining a following even then. During their conversation on the phone that day, Jimmy Ray told him he'd worked as a DJ at radio stations in Memphis, Nashville and Charlotte, among other places.

"You like living in Charlotte?" Pete asked.

Jimmy Ray's face clouded over. "Not there anymore. Working at a station in Wilson now."

Pete frowned. "Where's that?"

"A little way from Charlotte. The station was looking for a DJ and I needed a change."

The dark expression on Jimmy Ray's face told him there was more to the story than his desire for change. He didn't pry, but did note, "Sometimes change is good."

Jimmy Ray's face continued to look troubled. "So they say. Anyway, we got a new station manager in Charlotte. A real prick."

"How so?"

"Accused me of being a lousy DJ and screwing his wife."

"Not you," Pete said with mock innocence.

Jimmy Ray noticed Pete's expression and said indignantly, "Don't give me that look. Maybe I slept with her once or twice, but nothing regular, and no more than other guys. The manager was just out to get me, that's all. I was too big for him."

Pete stifled a laugh and they sat quietly for a few minutes. Then Jimmy Ray said, "That Roy Orbison could really play. I remember jamming with him while I was at that station in Memphis. Later on, he tried to talk me into giving up the DJ business and going on the road with him. But playing the music was always the thing that got my dick throbbing so I said 'no.'"

"Mmm," Pete murmured, thinking about dates. "So after you got out," he said as an aside, "you continued to play in addition to being a DJ?"

"Oh, hell yeah. I was pretty good, too, or Roy wouldn't have asked me to play with him." He paused and looked thoughtful. "Good man, that Roy Orbison. Not like some of those guys in the business. He knew he could count on me. Every new tune he came out with, I was always the first to play it on the air. Played his old stuff, too. That kept his career going at a time when he otherwise would have faded. That's the business for you. Always some new hot shot coming along nipping at your heels. Same thing with the DJ world."

"When did Roy Orbison ask you to go on the road with him?" Pete asked

Jimmy Ray thought for a while. "I don't remember exactly. It was after 1994, that I do recall. That's the year I got divorced from Caroline. Maybe 1995 or 1996?"

That can't be, Pete thought. Roy Orbison died of a heart attack in 1988. He decided to just let Jimmy Ray's story pass although the thought of him playing with the great Roy Orbison was a huge joke. He remembered their days together in Nürnberg. Jimmy Ray had a guitar then, but he was, in a word, terrible. Dickie Aug would look at Pete while Jimmy

Ray laboriously picked his way through an old Eddie Arnold tune and roll his eyes. They were always grateful when he went back to what he was really good at, playing the music rather than making it.

"So after you left Memphis," Pete said, "you went to Nashville and then Charlotte."

"Yeah, they were all big venues, and I worked my way to the top of all of them. Funny thing, the truly great music never grows old or stale. It's not like some of this new shit. These days, songs rise to the top of the charts and then fade just as fast. But a few guys have what it takes to stay up there. Roy Orbison is one. Johnny Cash was another." He looked pensive for a minute. "Jesus, I would have given anything to be at San Quentin when Johnny recorded 'Folsom Prison Blues.' They say the cons were so worked up that the guards just stayed back and let them howl. When he sang that line about shooting a man in Reno just to watch him die, I guess the place damn near imploded."

"Yeah," Pete said. "That must have been something. They didn't call him the 'Man in Black' for nothing."

"Amen, brother, amen. Let me see what else you got in this collection of yours."

He started sorting through Pete's CD collection again. After a while, he turned back to Pete and said, "Seeing all these Fats Domino CDs makes me a little sad. You must have a dozen or more."

"Fifteen, I think," Pete said, "but why does that make you sad?"

"Fats was one of my all-time favorites," Jimmy Ray replied. "Until I found out what a lying, cheating sonofabitch he was."

Pete looked at him sharply. Fats Domino was a rock and roll icon whose music virtually created the genre before Elvis and some of those other guys came along. Pete first heard of him when Jimmy Ray used to play his stuff in their army days.

Jimmy Ray slid a CD into the player and the distinctive sounds of "The Fat Man" came drifting out. You could hear Fats doing "wah-wah" as his accompaniment provided a strong back beat. Jimmy Ray turned up the sound and played along on air piano. He closed his eyes as if in a trance. When he opened them again, he said, "That fat bastard knew how to caress a song, that's for sure." "The Fat Man" was Domino's first hit and was credited with selling over a million records.

"That he could," Pete replied. "Even at his age, he sounds damn good."

"He *sounded* damn good," Jimmy Ray corrected him.

"Huh?"

"He died just before Katrina hit, remember?"

Pete noted the serious expression on Jimmy Ray's face. What was he talking about? First Roy Orbison, and now Fats Domino. He had them exactly turned around. Roy was dead and Fats was alive. He distinctly remembered all the television coverage after Katrina. Fats and his family were feared dead until a reporter broke the story that they'd been rescued by the Coast Guard. A little later, he remembered seeing Fats on television with President Bush in a highly-publicized visit the President made to New Orleans.

Getting his facts mixed up on Roy Orbison was one thing, but doing the same with Fats Domino was almost too much. Pete said, as delicately as he could manage, "I seem to recall all the publicity when Fats and his family were saved from the flooding that came with Katrina. And if I'm not mistaken,

Fats appeared on television with President Bush when he gave him that medal to replace the one President Clinton had given him."

Jimmy Ray looked at Pete for a long time and his eyes took on that strange glow again. "You're wrong, there, Pete. Fats met his Maker *before* the hurricane."

Pete furled his brow again. "That's funny. I could swear ...."

Jimmy Ray interrupted him. "You must be thinking of someone else."

He must have noticed the skeptical look on Pete's face because he added, "Fats is dead. I should know." He paused for a moment, then looked Pete in the eye. "Maybe I should tell you," he said quietly. "I'm the one who killed him."

A jolt shot through Pete's body when he heard Jimmy Ray's words. What the hell was he talking about? Fats not only wasn't dead, he was the poster boy for the resiliency of New Orleans. But here was his old army buddy claiming he'd killed Fats Domino.

Jimmy Ray continued, "I know it comes as a shock. Maybe I should explain." He paused again. "You ever been to New Orleans, Pete?"

"A few times," Pete said slowly.

"How about the Garden District? A restaurant called Louie's, you ever been there?"

Pete shook his head.

"Best food in New Orleans. Antoine's and them other tourist places, they can't hold a candle to Louie's. Satch and all those dudes, they want a great meal, they go to Louie's. There's no connection between Satch and the restaurant, by the way. It's just a coincidence they have the same name."

Pete continued to look at Jimmy Ray and said nothing.

"I first met Fats in 1996," Jimmy Ray went on. "His agent at the time was Sidney Rosenbloom. Sid used to call on me every now and again and pump Fats' stuff. Fats was past his hey day — you know, 'Ain't That a Shame,' 'Blueberry Hill,' big hits like that — but he was still recording. Sid wanted to keep his music alive. Royalties and all that played a part, of course, but I think Sid genuinely liked Fats. Me, I thought Fats made damn good music."

Jimmy Ray looked out the window again at the fishing shacks on the frozen lake. A snowmobile with two men aboard was powering out to one of the shacks.

"That sure does look like fun. They catch anything when it's this cold?"

"Sure," Pete replied. "They catch a lot of fish if you can stand to sit in one of those little shacks drinking schnapps and freezing your buns off. You were saying about Fats...."

"I'd like to try that sometime," Jimmy Ray said. "One of those little houses yours?"

"No," Pete answered, "I'm not one for ice fishing. I know some guys who have shacks out there, though. If you want, I'll see if we can use one of them so you can try your luck before you leave."

"That would be great. That would really give me something to talk about with my friends down South. Maybe we could get a closer look at that grave site at the same time."

"I'll see what I can arrange. You were telling me about Fats."

"Yeah, right, Fats. Anyway, one day Sid says to me, 'How'd you like to meet Fats?'" Jimmy Ray grunted and shook his head at the memory. Pete waited impatiently for him to continue.

"Anyway, at the time, I was going to be in New Orleans for a DJ convention so I said, 'Sure.' We wound up having dinner at Louie's. That's how I met Fats. We really hit it off. I saw him maybe once or twice a year after that, always in New Orleans and always for dinner at Louie's. You know why Fats didn't like to travel outside New Orleans? Said New Orleans was the only place he could get a good meal. And Fats loved his food. Man, that dude could eat!

"We got into a routine after a couple of years. One time I would buy, the next time he would buy, and so on. There was never any disagreement. It was kind of a natural thing, a gentlemen's agreement. Then one night I was in New Orleans the summer of Katrina and Fats, Sid and I decided to have dinner. Louie knew we were coming and arranged for us to dine in the kitchen. You ever do that, Pete? They set up a table in the kitchen and you can watch the food being prepared and everything. It was special. A dab of this, a dab of that. Shrimp prepared eight different ways. You ever have a dinner like that, where a world-class chef prepares dishes specially for you?"

"Once," Pete replied, "at a place in Chicago. Won it at a charity raffle."

"Well, you know what I'm talking about, then. I tell you, it was something. Three hours. That's how long it took us to finish our meal. We topped it off with some kind of Cajun desert. Man, I thought I'd gone to Heaven.

"It was late by the time we finished. Close to midnight, as I recall, and the place was nearly empty. Louie is funny. New Orleans is a late night town, but midnight and he closes down. That's just the way it is even though it's New Orleans."

Pete was waiting for Jimmy Ray to get to the punch line, to tell him it was all a big joke. Tell him he'd never met Fats Domino, that he'd never been to New Orleans. But Jimmy Ray continued.

"Anyway, Louie brings the bill. That dinner wasn't cheap, I tell you. Louie put it in the middle of the table like he always did, and even though it was Fats' turn to buy, he didn't reach for it. After a while, I nudged the bill toward him. He just pushed it back toward me. I replayed everything in my mind and was convinced I was right, that it was Fats' turn to buy. 'I think it's your turn to buy, Fats,' I said and shoved the bill back. Fats just shook his head and pushed the bill over to my side of the table again. 'Your turn,' he said. He had a scowl on his face I'd never seen before and I could tell he was dug in.

"If there's one thing I can't stand it's a piker, and right then and there my opinion of Fats Domino changed. I'm sitting at the table, trying to figure out what to do. Then I see Fats put his hand under this baggy shirt he was wearing. His eyes were like a dead man's. That old Johnny Cash song, the one we were talking about? Did you know that Fats was a Johnny Cash fan? He was and many times I'd heard him talk about that scene, watching a man dying and all. That flashed through my mind, too, and then I see this object in his hand. Looked like a gun. Jesus, I thought, he's got a piece! Anyway, I was carrying at the time — legal, too, since some guy who thought I was banging his wife was stalking me — and I decided I wasn't going to go down at the hands of a guy who reneged on his dinner obligation. I pulled out my own weapon and squeezed. I swear, I just meant to wing him, but the round caught him square in the chest."

Jimmy Ray sat back in his chair. "Fats died before the ambulance got there. You know what that object in his hand was? Some damn voodoo thing. Voodoo, for crissakes! You know Fats was born French. At least that's what he grew up speaking. I don't know whether he was going to put the hex on me, or what. I immediately felt bad about what happened, I really did. But none of it was my fault. Louie and Sid even agreed it wasn't my fault. That's kind of a long way of telling how I know Fats is dead."

Pete just stared at him for a few moments. "Jimmy Ray, you forget that I'm a lawyer. Even if my memory is faulty about seeing Fats on television after Katrina, do you expect me to believe that you shot a man in cold blood in front of witnesses and just walked away from the whole thing? No prison time, nothing?"

"Pete, Pete, listen. I didn't just walk away. There was an investigation, sure, but in the end, they concluded I was justified."

"On what grounds?"

Jimmy Ray got that strange look in his eyes again. He leaned forward and said, "What are all of our laws based on?"

"What do you mean?"

"I'll help you out," Jimmy Ray said. "The common laws of England ring a bell?"

"Sure, but you're not going to tell me the common law of England lets you shoot a man over a dinner tab."

"Not the common laws of England. But there's an exception to the derivation of our laws, which is…." He snapped his fingers a couple of times. "What state is New Orleans in?"

"Louisiana," Pete replied.

"Louisiana. Bingo. The old Napoleonic Code, right? You don't practice down there, and you said you don't do criminal work, so I wouldn't expect you to know this, but they have a lot of defenses, many of them built around heat of passion. Some of them have food as a focus because food is so damn important down there. Part of their culture. After the police finished investigating, they concluded that the heat of passion defense over food applied in my case. That and the fact I had a genuine belief that Fats had a gun. As I said, Louie and Sid backed up my story. They thought he had a weapon, too."

Pete wasn't sure what to say. No question that Louisiana had a civil law system, and that it differed in some respects from the laws of other states. But a defense involving heat of passion over food...?

"Jimmy Ray, all of the stuff I told you about Fats happened *after* the time you say you shot him. To cap it off, he gave a concert that was televised a couple of years ago. He certainly didn't look dead to me."

Jimmy Ray just shook his head like Pete was the dumbest guy to come down the pike all year. "You ever hear of look-alikes?" he asked. "There are plenty of African-Americans who live in New Orleans who look exactly like Fats. That's probably what you saw. Was the man really singing or was he mouthing the words? You can't say, can you?"

Pete thought about that for a moment. "I'm not saying I don't believe you," he said, "but except for performing, there's nothing Fats' agent couldn't do if Fats were dead instead of alive. Sell CDs, peddle tee-shirts, and so on. Why would Sid want to hide the fact Fats was dead and how did he hope to pull it off?"

Jimmy Ray shook his head again for about the sixth time. "Some people are better off commercially if they're alive and some people are better off commercially if they're dead. Take Elvis, for example…."

"Oh for God's sake, Jimmy Ray, you're not going to tell me one of those Elvis sighting stories, are you?"

The gleam returned to Jimmy Ray's eyes. "I know it's hard to believe. I used to be a skeptic, too." He paused for a moment and then continued. "You probably don't have a Winn-Dixie store around here, do you? Well, down South it's different. Down where I live, there's a Winn-Dixie on every corner. Plenty of folks have seen Elvis in back of one of their stores waiting for an employee to bring food out to him."

"I have heard those stories," Pete replied sarcastically. "They're usually on the front page of the *National Enquirer* or the *Star* or some other supermarket tabloid. I don't know anyone who believes those stories unless they're conspiracy theorists."

"It's not just conspiracy theorists, I can tell you. I told you, I was as skeptical about some of that bull as anyone. Then late one night, I happened to be at a Winn-Dixie, and as I was leaving, I saw a man out back who was the spitting image of Elvis. I watched with my mouth open. A guy came out the back door of the store, handed him a package, and went inside again. It was Elvis, I tell you. I saw it with my own eyes. Elvis just couldn't take all the pressure of being an idol anymore, so he and a couple of others faked his death."

"Why Winn-Dixie?" Pete asked disbelievingly.

"As the story goes, the CEO of that chain was a huge Elvis fan. Apparently he was in on his fake death. Then there's the management group. There's kind of a secret society at Winn-Dixie, people in the know tell me. You only rise above a certain level there if you buy into the Elvis death thing. They're totally committed to the King. Make sure he's provided food and all that. You can believe it or not, but I tell you, I'm in the business and people confide things in me."

"Same question, Jimmy Ray. Why would Elvis want to fake his own death?"

"Couldn't take the pressure any more," Jimmy Ray replied with a confident air. "Had a strong desire to live, but couldn't handle the pressure of being the biggest star in the music world. Can you imagine what that's like? Can't walk down the friggin' street without some babe wanting you to autograph her undies or asking for a snippet of hair. I tell you Pete, I've been pretty big in the music business myself and I know what it's like. And Elvis was a helluva lot bigger than me."

Jimmy Ray got up and walked over to Pete's CD collection again. Soon Johnny Cash came on, singing "Folsom Prison Blues."

"Listen to that," Jimmy Ray said. He got that gleam in his eyes again and mouthed the words about being able to hear the train outside the prison walls and the advice his momma had given him. When he got to the part about shooting a man in Reno just to watch him die, he repeated himself and said, "Shit, I would have given anything to be there when the Man in Black sang those words. I would have been howling and screaming along with the cons. I guess they worked themselves into a frenzy. Same kind of look I saw in Fats' eyes that night I shot him. Did I tell you about the voodoo thing Fats had in his hand? That thing I thought was a pistol? Well, Sid and I were out to dinner one night with Clemmie — that's the Fats look-a-like — and he told us there's a lot more to voodoo than people want to believe. Said I was damn lucky to get my shot in first because if the Fat Man had put the hex on me...."

CASH AFFAIR

The way Charlie Fain looked at it, a detective could lose his edge if he didn't take an occasional break from the grunt work that went with the job. Granted, that kind of thinking had gotten him into trouble in the past, but he'd become wiser since then, more resourceful.

Take his clap-trap old green Corolla. It didn't do much for his self-image, but he'd come to value the clunker for the simple reason that no one except the local scrap dealer ever gave it a second look. That made it perfect for times when he was tailing some bad guy. Or trying to leave a no-tell motel unnoticed at 4:58 in the afternoon.

Charlie scanned the parking lot as he headed toward the exit. Nothing moved. The red neon sign near the motel office, a chunk gouged from the fluted plastic, announced "cancy" to anyone interested. No need for repairs as long as the message was getting through. He thought about the credit card system that had been down again, and smiled. Cash had its advantages.

Six fast food joints west on the frontage road, he pulled into a seedy strip mall and parked at the far end. He stretched to loosen his back muscles. A couple of hours with Angie made him feel like he'd just played in one of those over-forty rugby games down in Lincoln Park. After three straight days of investigating third-rate burglaries, though, it had been a nice morale boost.

The problem was that his new boss, the crusty Chief-of-Police in west suburban Springdale, could care less about his morale, or that he had been the toast of the Chicago PD only two years earlier for solving the Bucktown serial murder case. Instead, the old bird watched his every move like a falcon circling its prey. That's why Charlie had been careful to stick his head in several area pawnshops and secondhand stores before rushing to meet Angie. He pulled out a small notebook and recorded a few details of those visits. It wasn't much; a little creative report writing would be required when he got to the station.

Charlie checked his cell phone. Eight messages. Four from the Chief, the last about 30 minutes ago. He groaned. He'd heard the cell phone play his signature Bolero a couple of times while he was right in the middle of things with Angie. An appropriate tune, he'd thought at the time, and no way he was going to take a call then. Not with her whispering in his ear that he was the best. A helluva lot different than his ex who'd overlooked no opportunity to let him know he was the world's biggest bust in bed and out.

He slid a flask from under the passenger seat and took a long swig of Stoli. He was a Jack Daniels man, but had switched to vodka during the day because it was less noticeable. He felt the liquid warm his body and sighed. Times certainly had changed. When he started out 20 years ago, everyone had a pop or two at lunch, and maybe a little something in the afternoon as well. But now people treated you like some wino if you even looked at the stuff. He wasn't an alcoholic, he knew that, but he had thought about maybe checking out one of those AA programs just to see what they were all about. But when did he have the time?

He took another swallow and played back the Chief's first message.

"Charlie, we got a problem at 492 Elm. Call me."

The second call had come 15 minutes later. At an amped-up decibel level. "Dammit, Charlie, call me back and do it now! A guy just got whacked in his own bedroom! I need you over here!"

The last two messages were somewhat more emphatic just in case the urgency hadn't been clear from the others.

Charlie braced himself for what he knew was coming and punched the Chief's number.

"Chief, Charlie here. Got your messages. I'm on my way."

"Where the hell have you been?" the Chief bellowed. "I've been calling you for over an hour!"

"Sorry," Charlie said, holding the phone away from his ear. "I had to change a tire and my cell battery was low."

"Well, get over here! I don't care if you have to run!"

"I'll be there in 10 minutes, Chief." He hit the red button before another sonic boom could permanently impair his hearing.

Charlie grimaced. It was cover your butt time. He chewed half a pack of Lifesavers, and to mask the peppermint, wolfed down two stale Twinkies he'd promised himself not to eat. Then he checked his clothes and adjusted his shirt so the placket lined up with the one on his khaki pants. A glance in the rearview mirror showed no signs of the afternoon's activity except for his hair; he took care of that with a few strokes of a brush. Satisfied that he looked good enough to greet royalty, he headed for Elm Street, light flashing on the Corolla's dash.

He could hardly believe there'd been a shooting in his leafy little suburb. Maybe it was partly due to the Stoli, but his adrenaline was flowing for the first time in months. It was almost like the old days when he was Dan Considine's guy at the Chicago PD and they were out busting perps left and right. Until some jealous yahoos in the department started spreading rumors and did him in, that is.

When he arrived at 492 Elm, black and whites were everywhere. Outdoor floods illuminated the imposing house with white neoclassical columns in front; it screamed new money from every cornice and cupola. He felt a little depressed when he thought of his own crummy apartment building, but took solace in the fact that the yellow crime-scene tape gave the grand place a comical touch. Made it look a little like a high school prom queen's house after a good tepeeing with toilet paper by the senior boys.

Charlie was so mesmerized by the scene that he'd been slow to realize he was looking at Angie's house. Damn! He thought when the realization hit him. He scrambled from the car and elbowed his way through the mass of gawkers standing six deep along the sidewalk, wondering what quirk of fate had led to a shooting at the home of a woman he'd just spent the afternoon with in the sack. Angie couldn't have been involved, though, given the time of the Chief's messages.

He ran smack into the Chief the moment he stepped into the foyer. As usual, the old boy looked like something right out of an ad in *Law Enforcement Today*. His spotless blue uniform, fringe of white hair and neatly-trimmed mustache gave him a distinguished if jowly look. Charlie didn't have to look twice to figure out his mood.

"Nice of you to make it, Fain." If his words had been any frostier, they would have required an ice bucket.

"Sorry, Chief. I told you what happened. Where's the body?"

"C'mon." The Chief started down the hall with the stride of a man 20 years younger, but after a few steps spun around and poked his face to within a foot of Charlie's.

"What's wrong with your eyes?" He studied Charlie as though he were searching for scratches on the department's shiny new Crown Vic cruiser. "You been drinking?"

Charlie donned his best falsely accused look. "No, why?"

"Your eyes look like crap. You look like you've been drinking."

"Must be from this stuff," Charlie said, holding out his hands so the Chief could see the grime. "I think I got some in my eyes." He'd anticipated being grilled by the Chief, so as a precaution, he'd rubbed his hands on the spare tire and let out the air before leaving the strip mall. Attention to detail, his stock in trade.

The Chief continued to stare at him. "You know our understanding, Charlie. I catch you drinking on the job or pulling any of your other shenanigans and you're gone. You're here only as a favor to Considine. No second chances."

"I understand," Charlie said. "Now where's the body?"

The Chief gave him one last skeptical look, then turned and continued down the hall.

When they reached the bedroom, Charlie craned his neck to see around the photographer snapping pictures of the crime scene. A stocky man lay face down on the floor. He was naked except for a thick towel knotted around his waist, unless the clunky gold chain and pinky ring the size of an oyster counted as items of apparel. His fleshy back had more fur than the average suburban raccoon. Blood soaked the carpet around his head and chest and had turned dark as it dried. A handgun lay nearby.

Charlie glanced around the room. Forty feet long at least, and with the lights turned up, so bright it made him want to reach for his shades. Except for the blood stains, everything was white. Walls, bedspread, shag carpet. Charlie shook his head. Who had white shag carpet these days? He visualized Angie stretched out on the massive four-poster bed but tried to put the thought out of his mind and moved closer to the young, carrot-topped evidence technician crouched near the handgun. It looked like a small caliber Ruger.

"How many times was he shot?" Charlie asked.

"Seven," the tech said. "Chest looks like a sieve. Two to the head."

Charlie exhaled through pursed lips. "I guess that rules out suicide."

The tech's freckled face crinkled in a toothy grin. "Unless he had an awfully high pain threshold and wanted to be sure to finish the job." When the Chief approached, still looking snarly as hell, the tech quickly resumed his work.

"Well," the Chief said, looking at Charlie, "any observations?"

"For starters, it's probably a clean piece so the gunman could just dump it. I assume the vic is Mr. Pavia, right?"

The Chief nodded and shifted his gaze back toward the body.

Charlie needed to get up to speed on the facts. "Was anyone else home?" he asked, having first-hand knowledge that the vic's wife hadn't been.

"Not that we know of," the Chief said. "The neighbor lady called it in. She heard the dog going nuts and called 911 when no one answered the door."

"What's the dog's name?" Charlie asked. "Lassie?" He caught the Chief's eye and grinned.

"How the hell would I know the dog's name?" the Chief said. From his glare, it was clear that he either wasn't an old movie buff or didn't appreciate Charlie's brand of humor. "I guess you've seen a lot of this, huh? Doesn't seem to bother you much."

The Chief was right, Charlie thought, he had seen a lot of it. Probably too much. He stared at the blood stains near the body. "No," he said to the Chief, "it bothers me."

A woman's voice shrieked from down the hall "Let me through! This is my house, dammit!"

Charlie turned and saw a woman struggling to get past two uniformed officers. Not just any woman; Angie Pavia, with whom he'd just spent two hours in the sack. Her blouse pulled open during the struggle. Charlie knew he shouldn't be thinking about her boobs at a time like this, but damn, it was hard not to.

Angie broke free from the officers and raced down the hall. Her cheeks were flushed and her eyes looked disoriented. The Chief, showing surprising agility for a man of his age and bulk, jumped into her path. "Mrs. Pavia, don't go in there." He placed a hand on her arm.

"Get away from me!" Angie screamed. "What happened?!!" She brushed off the Chief's hand like a bothersome gnat and pushed through to the bedroom door. She gasped at the sight of her husband's body, then sank to her knees, hands clutched to her face. "Oh my God! Oh my God!" Her body jerked with each sob.

Charlie felt awkward and just a little helpless. Taking her in his arms and comforting her somehow didn't seem like the prudent thing to do just then. So he watched. As she continued to sob, he was impressed by the outpouring of grief from a woman who didn't exactly lead a monogamous life. And he felt a little uncomfortable when she glanced at him a couple of times between sobs.

■ ■ ■

Charlie was pumped despite some nagging concerns over how he was going to keep his dalliance with Angie under wraps while investigating her husband's murder. But finally a real case. He leaned back in his chair and propped his feet on one corner of the Chief's desk. The Chief eyed his detective's shoes and his mouth twitched as though he were about to say something.

"Okay," Charlie said, getting right to it, "here's what we know. According to the medical examiner, the vic was shot sometime around three, give or take a half hour. That squares with when the neighbor lady heard the dog. Other occupants of the house were his wife and her 20-something son. As far as we know, neither was home that afternoon."

"The kid's not the vic's son, right?" the Chief asked.

"Right," Charlie said. "He's Mrs. Pavia's child by her second marriage."

The Chief stopped picking at a fingernail and looked up. "She's been married three times?"

"That we know of. Anyway, no one we've talked to so far reports noticing anything unusual until the dog went wild. The patio door was forced. That's probably how the perp got in. No prints on the weapon. Serial number was ground off just as we expected, and ballistics hasn't come up with anything."

The Chief squinted at Charlie. "If someone was going to blow away a guy, why would he use a popgun like that .22 caliber Ruger?"

"Not clear. Professionals sometimes use small caliber weapons."

"You saying this might have been a hit?" the Chief asked.

"Possible. No sign robbery was the motive. The shot pattern doesn't look like a pro, but maybe the vic rushed him and that caused it."

The Chief grunted and fixed Charlie with one of his stares. "Why did Mrs. Pavia keep looking at you that day?"

Wonderful, Charlie thought, old eagle eyes had noticed. He shrugged, trying to act casual. "No idea."

"You're saying you don't know her?"

"Right," Charlie said, feeling a little damp under his arms.

The Chief walked across the room and filled his cup from a glass coffee pot resting on a hotplate. He raised the pot and looked at Charlie. "You want some?"

Charlie's stomach churned at the sight of the sludge that remained. He waved off the Chief's offer and dropped his feet to the floor. After a good stretch, he rubbed one shoulder. Must still be feeling the effects of Angie, he thought, as he leaned back in the chair. Or maybe just getting old.

Seizing the opportunity, the Chief grabbed a cloth and polished the spot on his desk Charlie had been using as a footrest. Then he stood there like a sentinel, apparently out of concern that Charlie might try to resume his former position.

"I want you on this full time," the Chief finally said. "We need to make an arrest before the village trustees get on me. And I don't want the state boys or feds sticking their noses into this if we can avoid it. Keep control of the investigation if you can."

Charlie nodded. "I understand."

"By the way," the Chief said, "Considine called. Asked how you were doing."

Charlie raised an eyebrow. The Chief talking to Considine about him was never a good thing. "And?" he asked.

"Told him the jury was still out."

Charlie took that as a cue to leave before the Chief could start again about his precarious job status. He hurried out of the Chief's office and walked to the parking lot and studied the old Corolla. It looked even worse than usual in the October sunshine. Charlie thought about his sporty little Miata convertible housed safely back in his apartment's garage. It had been a gift to himself after the divorce, but was just too flashy for work. Still, he was tempted to go home, swap cars, and go for a spin on what was likely one of the last nice days of the season. Good judgment prevailed and he slid into the Corolla and forced himself to do something he'd been putting off — call Angie.

"Thanks for calling right away to express your condolences, you poop," she said upon hearing his voice.

"The Chief's been running me ragged," Charlie said. "But I really am sorry about Carmen."

"Don't be," came the matter-of-fact reply. "He was a jerk."

Charlie was taken aback. "Are you trying to tell me something?"

"Just the truth," she said. "But a terrible crime was committed and you have to find the killer."

"That's why I'm calling," he said. "What can you tell me about Carmen's business partners?"

"Partner. Herbie Klein. Disgusting creature. Looks like a toad. He was always trying to use the company for dirty things he was involved in."

Okay, Charlie thought, that fit with rumors he'd heard about Carmen's associates. "Carmen objected?" he asked.

"Yes," she said, "they had fights over it."

"Do you think Herbie had something to do with Carmen's murder?"

"I know he did. You should arrest him."

Vintage Angie. No shades of gray in her world. "How can I reach Herbie?" he asked.

"Call P&K Realty in Cicero."

"Thanks," Charlie said. "Well, I've…."

"When am I going to see you?"

So much for business. Charlie had hoped Angie would be sufficiently shaken by Carmen's murder that she wouldn't try to restoke the fires with him. At least not yet. The last thing he needed was to have her pressuring him for a repeat performance right in the middle of his investigation. Concealing one afternoon with her was going to be challenging enough.

"I'll call you soon," he said.

"Promise? You're not worried about someone finding out about us, are you? Would you be in trouble?"

"No, no," Charlie said, "I'll call you."

He signed off before Angie could prolong the conversation. He thought back to how she'd honed in on him that night at the bar a few weeks ago. When he'd asked how she knew he was with the department, she'd just smiled and said every woman knew when a new stud arrived in town. Charlie liked the stud part, but had sensed the woman was trouble and should have stayed away. He hadn't and now he had a problem. He got the feeling Angie knew it, too.

Charlie arrived on time at Petros, an all-night joint in an industrial area a few miles south of Springdale. It was one of those places where $6.95 would get you a four egg omelette, a slab of ham, your choice of hash browns or three pancakes, and a dollop of fruit cocktail straight from the can. No extra charge for the grease.

He settled into a booth in the rear. A spandex-clad waitress with enough mascara and eyeliner to make Tammy Faye Baker envious appeared and tried to interest him in conversation or food, in that order. Charlie put her off as diplomatically as he could; it was a work night. When he was finally alone, he sipped a cup of black coffee and waited for his snitch to appear. He checked his watch. Miguel was already a half-hour late.

A rail-thin young Hispanic man with blotchy skin, stringy black hair pulled back in a pony tail and a heavy gold earring finally walked in and made his way toward the rear of the restaurant. The collar of his dirty denim jacket shielded the sides of his face, and his eyes darted about as he passed through the room.

"Hey, man," Miguel whispered as he slid into the booth opposite Charlie, "I know I owe you and everything. But you need to promise not to let it out that we talked, okay? This gets around the street...."

Charlie raised his hand. "You do owe me, Mig, and I'm glad you remember that even if you can't remember the time. But I'll keep you out of it if I can. Now what do you have?"

Miguel didn't look fully convinced by Charlie's assurances, but said in a low voice, "I checked around. Guy in Berwyn who deals in a lot of stuff you don't want to know about says he sold a clean Ruger to a guy a couple of weeks ago."

"Who bought it?" Charlie asked.

Miguel shrugged. "Some dude."

Charlie had passed on busting Miguel a couple of times, and the *quid pro quo* was for him to provide information. It was payback time.

"Listen, friend, I need a name or you've got problems with Chicago PD. Some people on the street may be interested in your activities, too."

"Aw, man, why you doing this?" He glanced nervously about and his mouth twitched. After a pause, he whispered, "Everyone calls him Junior, that's all I know."

"Junior?" Charlie asked.

"Some stinkin' Pole. Real psychopath." Miguel made eye contact with Charlie for the first time. "You must be out of touch, man. They say he's already whacked seven stiffs. Even the made guys are scared of him."

Charlie stared at him. "You have a last name or description?"

Miguel picked at a loose thread on his jacket sleeve and shrugged again. "Those 'ski' names all sound alike, you know?" Then he added, "Tall, real skinny, my guy said. Pale skin like he don't never go out in the sun. Wears these big glasses that make him look like some damn geek."

"Anything else?" Charlie asked.

Miguel gave his usual shrug. "My guy said he was crappin' his pants because he'd heard about this Junior dude from other people. Didn't want to upset him or nothin'. He looked real jumpy, you know? Dude bought the first piece my guy showed him and split. Didn't even ask for no ammo."

"Thanks, Mig," Charlie said, filing away the information. "You did good after you got over your temporary loss of memory."

"Are we square now, Charlie?"

"Not exactly, but you made a pretty nice down payment."

■ ■ ■

Florence Mabry wrinkled her nose when Charlie asked about the Pavias. "We're just neighbors; we don't socialize," she said, fussing with her tight bun. "I'm old Springdale, you know. I was the only one that wouldn't sell to that developer who tore down all the nice homes around our lake." She lowered her voice. "The word is that Mr. Pavia paid off some people to get the zoning. Their house is far too big for the lot, don't you think?"

Charlie grimaced and shook his head to show his own disgust.

"You can learn a lot about people just by keeping your eyes and ears open," she continued. Her small, penetrating eyes darted about her orderly Victorian-style living room.

Watching her, Charlie got the feeling there wasn't much that she missed. "You'd make an excellent detective, Mrs. Mabry," he said.

Her mouth curved into a little smile. "You can call me Florence, Charlie. I try not to snoop, but sometimes you can't help but notice things, you know?"

He nodded. "Anything specific?"

"They always argued." She lowered her voice again and leaned forward. "Have you met Mrs. Pavia? A lot of people don't think she's Springdale material, if you know what I mean. You should see how she dresses." Mrs. Mabry shook her head and put a hand to her dress collar as though to reassure herself it was firmly fastened at the neck.

"Umm," Charlie murmured. "What did they argue about?"

"Money, usually." Her eyes gleamed. "Mrs. Pavia is a big spender."

"Okay," Charlie said. "How about the son?"

"Claims he's in the technology business, but all he does is help people hook up their computers." She gave a little snort. "Spends most of his time trying to imitate famous people. That and practice his magic tricks."

Charlie thought for a moment. That would explain the life-sized posters of John Wayne, Mark Twain and other celebrities he'd seen on Mason's bedroom walls the day of the murder. He could just see the kid doing his Duke Wayne routine: "Look, pilgrim, you're about to get a good dose of lead poison. But first, I'm going to pull a few bunnies out of your drawers."

"Did you see the son around the house the afternoon Carmen was shot?" Charlie asked.

"No," she said, looking a little put out, "but even I can't follow everything."

According to Mrs. Mabry, the only stranger she'd seen in the neighborhood that afternoon was a Greenpeace solicitor. When Charlie asked if he'd stopped at the Pavia house as well, her eyes widened. "He could have, Charlie. Maybe that's our man." She said he was tall and wore a tan jacket, blue jeans and bicycle helmet.

When they'd finished, Mrs. Mabry clasped his hand and said, "I know this is official police business, Charlie. No one will get a word out of me." She winked at him.

Charlie proceeded around the lake and knocked on doors until he found someone home. "I'm Charlie Fain," he said to the willowy, fiftyish brunette in tennis togs who greeted him on his third try. He flashed his badge. "I'm investigating Carmen Pavia's murder. Could I ask you a few questions?"

The woman examined the badge carefully and then let him in. The place was a clone of the Pavia mansion, except there wasn't a fiber of white shag carpet in sight. She told Charlie she'd been home the day Carmen was shot, but wasn't aware of what had happened until the police arrived.

"Did you notice anything unusual that afternoon?" Charlie asked.

She appeared to give his question some thought. "There was some guy poking around by the lake."

"Someone you recognized?"

She shook her head. "I was going to go out and ask him what he was doing, but then my daughter called. By the time I got off the phone, he was gone. I think I have a picture of him if you're interested."

Charlie raised his eyebrows. "A picture?"

"You know how we've had all of those burglaries this year?" she asked. "My friends and I decided we'd photograph any strangers we see in the neighborhood, just in case. I snapped him through the window while I was on the phone with Karen. Here, I'll show you."

She led Charlie into an upscale home office and he waited while she logged on a computer. "There he is," she said after a few minutes.

The monitor showed a picture of a tall man with large dark-framed eyeglasses and a baseball cap. He carried a fishnet. She pulled up a second photograph of the man taken from a different angle. At Charlie's request, she printed copies of both photographs for him.

Charlie thanked her and continued around the lake until he came to a small bench. He sat and stared at Angie's house for a few minutes. He knew he couldn't just avoid her; that might backfire if she became upset and pointed a finger at him out of spite. Besides, he needed information. He dialed her number.

"You calling to make a date?" she asked.

She was running true to form. "Not right now, I'm afraid," he said. "But I need to ask you a few more questions about Klein."

"You used to be a lot more fun, Charlie."

From the tone of her voice, she didn't seem to be kidding. That was a bad sign, but he ignored the comment. "Could you give me a description of Herbie?"

"Short and fat," Angie said. "And stupid."

"Okay," he said, laughing. "Do you know someone who's tall and thin and wears heavy, dark-rimmed glasses?"

There was a pause at the other end. "That sounds like the cadaver."

"Cadaver?" he asked.

"He works for Herbie. Ugly, ugly. Looks like he's back from the dead. He's probably the one who shot Carmen. You should arrest both of them."

Ms. black and white again, although her characterization of Junior seemed spot on with what Miguel had told him. "Have you met this cadaver fellow?" Charlie asked.

"He was at our house with Herbie. Gave me the creeps. I left and went shopping."

"Thanks," Charlie said, "that's very helpful. By the way, someone from the department will need to get additional statements from you and your son. Just for the record."

It took her a moment to respond. "Can't you take the statements?"

"The Chief decides those things," he said, taking liberties with the truth. "Our other detectives are good guys. You'll be okay with whoever you get. I can't say for sure, but a guy named Walton will probably be out to see you"

Earlier that day, Charlie had arranged for Kyle Walton, one of the department's detectives, to take the statements since there was no way he wanted to do it himself. Kyle couldn't find his butt with both hands, which made him perfect for the job as far as Charlie was concerned. It was going to be routine, anyway. He knew Angie hadn't killed Carmen, and the kid sounded like a flake. In other circumstances, he might have used Kathy Lopez, the third detective in the department, but she was too damn smart. No use taking a chance that she'd find some connection between him and Angie. The Chief had already picked up on the looks Angie had given him at the murder scene.

Charlie sat in Herbie Klein's office a couple of hours later, listening to him lament the tragedy of Carmen's death. Brown leatherette furniture filled the office, and landscape prints of the kind sold by K-Mart framed and ready to hang for $39.95 adorned the walls. A large aquarium shared one corner with a plastic ficus.

Herbie introduced Charlie to one of his business associates, a man named Ludoslaw Ostrowski, and asked whether he could join them. It was a no brainer as soon as Charlie saw the beanpole with heavy, dark-rimmed glasses and a weathered baseball cap. He was, as law enforcement officials like to say, a person of interest in the murder investigation. With a name like Ludoslaw Ostrowski, Charlie could see why someone had hung the "Junior" moniker on him. Probably not to his face, though.

"How long were you partners with Carmen Pavia?" Charlie asked.

"Fourteen years." Herbie sighed. "I don't know what I'm going to do without him. We were like brothers." Herbie walked across the office and stared at the aquarium. After a minute or two, he tossed in some live bait and giggled like a schoolboy after his first feel as the small fish — probably piranha — ripped away at it.

Lovely guy, Charlie thought. "What happens to the business now?" he asked.

Herbie finally got himself under control and shrugged. "I've got to buy out his estate. Probably means I'll have to sell some damn good properties to raise cash."

"Can't you just continue in business with his widow?" Charlie asked.

Herbie looked even more like a toad when he grinned. "That bimbo?" he said. "Carmen wouldn't let her near the business with a 10-foot pole. Said she'd burn through everything in six months."

Throughout the conversation, Junior had sat motionless like some pasty-skinned mannequin. The only time he even twitched was when he'd nodded almost imperceptibly to confirm that he'd been with Klein looking at some property 50 miles to the north at the time Carmen Pavia was murdered. His pale, dead eyes remained glued to Charlie like a Sidewinder missile locked on the exhaust of an enemy jet. Charlie had dealt with a lot of bad dudes, but something about Junior made him especially uneasy. Probably was a helluva real estate man, though. Made all kinds of offers that others couldn't refuse.

Charlie could feel Junior's eyes on his back as he walked to the Corolla. He took a swallow of Stoli, exited the P&K parking lot and punched Dan Considine's number at Chicago PD. Dan confirmed that Junior was indeed on their radar screen and had every bit the reputation Miguel had ascribed to him. He'd been booked several times, Dan said, but never indicted. Before signing off, Charlie thanked Dan once again for his help in getting him the Springdale job. Dan, hardly an angel himself, gave Charlie his standard lecture about staying on the straight and narrow.

Most of the evidence pointed to Junior, Charlie thought, as he drove past rows of cookie-cutter bungalows on his way back to Springdale. Probably was doing Herbie Klein's bidding just like Angie had said. The bicycle solicitor Mrs. Mabry and another neighbor had seen was a second potential suspect. According to Greenpeace, though, none of their people had been working the Pavia's neighborhood that day. Maybe the killer had been posing as a representative for cover. Maybe, but there were a lot of things about the case that bothered him.

■ ■ ■

Mort's Partytime billed itself as Chicagoland's leading source of costumes for all occasions. Charlie admired a Dracula outfit, complete with a red-lined cape, and considered buying it for the Halloween party he planned to attend with some of his old Chicago PD buddies. He also kept an eye on a gang of aspiring young ghosts, goblins and witches as they eagerly outfitted themselves for the big night. He refrained from suggesting that they ask for Junior costumes if they wanted to be really scary.

While waiting for Mort, Charlie flipped though Kyle Walton's report on his interview with Angie's son, Mason. As expected, it contained no revelations. Mason said he'd made some service calls that morning, and then had spent the afternoon scoping out new computer products. He'd given the names of several stores he'd supposedly visited. Kyle didn't seem to have pushed him very hard on the details, which is about what he had expected.

Charlie checked his watch and called Kyle to get a quick report on his session with Angie. The conversation was interrupted when Mort finally broke free from his young customers. After making a sales pitch for the Dracula costume, Mort huddled with Charlie in a back office. A half hour later, Charlie was on his way to Tony's Sporting Goods, Dracula outfit on the seat beside him, to review some surveillance video tape. Boy, he thought, when he'd finished the eye-numbing exercise two hours later, being a homicide detective sure was exciting work. It had been a productive day, though, and he was feeling better about the case. And a little nervous, too.

Charlie's cell phone rang as he was pulling out of Tony's parking lot.

"Thanks for sending your attack dog, Mr. Walton, to grill me for two hours."

Charlie smiled. Maybe he needed to reassess his opinion of Kyle. "How did it go?" he asked solicitously.

"I told him he should be out looking for the killer," Angie said, "and not bothering a grieving widow."

"What did he ask? Where you were and things like that?"

She laughed. "Don't worry, darling, I didn't say a word about us."

"Mmm," Charlie murmured, feeling the same chill he always did when she got around to her favorite subject. After listening to her complain about Walton for 10 minutes, he said, "Angie, maybe we should get together. There are some things I'd like to talk to you about."

There was a pause at the other end. "I'm not doing anything now."

Charlie thought about it for a moment. Now was not exactly what he'd had in mind, but maybe it was just as well. "Okay," he said. "Where should we meet?"

"How about here? I'm alone. Mason is in Naperville with a friend."

He wasn't crazy about the idea, but didn't want to meet with her at the station and had no alternative to propose. "Fine," he said. "I need to wrap up a few things. I'll be over in an hour."

Charlie called Kyle Walton to finish their conversation. Nothing was brief with Kyle, and his head throbbed half-way through the ordeal. When he finally managed to get off the phone, he thought about the conversation for a moment and then laughed. He was still grinning when he walked into Kinko's 15 minutes later. After running some photocopies, he headed toward 492 Elm Street for what promised to be an interesting evening.

The door swung open as soon as he knocked and Angie greeted him with a lingering hug. She wore a blood-red silk blouse unbuttoned halfway down the front and pants that made her look like she'd been dipped to the waist in a vat of black paint. Business, he reminded himself.

"Let's go in here," Angie said, leading him into a study. "We don't want that busybody next door spying on us." Charlie agreed; he'd parked a block away to avoid Mrs. Mabry's prying eyes.

The wood-paneled room was furnished with the *de rigeur* black leather furniture and hunt scene prints. Charlie looked around while Angie got him a Jack and water. He doubted she would record their conversation, but reminded himself to be careful.

"I'm beginning to think you're right about this case," Charlie said after she'd returned with his drink.

She smiled. "You finally figured that out, huh?"

Charlie nodded. "A neighbor saw a man resembling your 'cadaver' friend by the lake the afternoon Carmen was shot. He's known as Junior, by the way. She took this picture." Charlie handed her a copy.

Angie studied the photograph. Her eyes were animated when she looked up. "That's him."

Charlie continued. "We've also located a guy who claims he sold a clean Ruger identical to the murder weapon a couple of weeks ago. From his description, the buyer sounds like Junior."

She gave him a smug look. "You should arrest Herbie Klein, too. I'm sure he was behind it just like I told you."

"Well," Charlie said, "he certainly had motive. Carmen and Herbie had disagreements, as you said. I also checked the partnership agreement and discovered that if one of them died, the survivor gets to buy out his estate at a discounted value. It was set up that way so the surviving partner wouldn't have to sell everything at fire-sale prices."

Angie's eyes widened. "You mean that fat toad is going to be able to screw me out of my money?"

"No, no," Charlie said. "You're going to get millions. Just not quite as much as if Carmen and Herbie had ended their partnership while both were still alive."

"So I'm just getting screwed a little," Angie said with a scowl on her face.

Charlie shrugged. "I didn't make the deal."

Angie walked over and sat on the arm of his chair. "You're very good, Charlie, and not just in bed. You probably need to relax after all your hard work." She placed a hand on his shoulder and let it snake down his chest.

He gave her hand a squeeze. "Do you mind if I get a refill?" He rose from his chair and walked to the bar and took his time fixing another Jack and water. Light on the Jack. A model of self-discipline.

"Are you coming back?" Angie asked in her throaty voice.

"I am," Charlie replied. "But before we get too comfortable, I need your thoughts on a few things."

"What things, darling?"

"For one, if Junior had intended to kill Carmen, why do you think he'd poke around the lake first where someone might see and be able to identify him?"

Her smile faded. "Maybe he likes to fish. Or maybe he's just stupid."

Charlie nodded. "Could be. But if you look closely at this photograph the neighbor took," he said, showing her an enlarged copy, "there seems to be hair sticking out from under the guy's baseball cap. Junior has some scalp condition and is completely bald."

Angie studied the photograph. "This is just a bad shot," she said. "That isn't hair. It's a reflection or something."

"I don't know," he said, "it looks like hair to me."

"Oh, come on, Charlie. He's your man. We both know it."

"Okay, then how do we explain this? The dealer who sold the gun said the buyer was real jumpy. Bought the first piece he showed him and couldn't wait to get out of there. That doesn't sound like the guy I met when I talked to Herbie. Junior hardly twitched for over an hour."

"Even I know that isn't evidence," Angie said. "Are we finished with all of this talk?" She tugged at his belt.

"Almost," Charlie said. "Just a question or two about Mason. I understand he does impressions of famous people. John Wayne, Buddy Holly...."

Angie stopped tugging and looked at him.

"You know," Charlie reminded her, "the old rock star? Dark hair, heavy dark-rimmed glasses?"

Angie's eyes narrowed. "Why are you asking about Mason?"

"I'm just thinking out loud about some things that are bothering me."

"I've been thinking, too," she said. Her tone was as icy as her eyes. "I hope you're attending to your job these days. Not doing what got you fired in Chicago."

Another shot across his bow. "Not an issue," he said, forcing a chuckle. "But Mason has a problem."

"Would you mind telling me why?" Angie said.

"I think he killed Carmen. They didn't get along and Mason knew you'd inherit a lot of money if he died."

"You're crazy!"

"I wish I was," Charlie said. "But when the gun dealer sees both Mason and Junior dressed the same, I believe he'll identify Mason as the buyer. We also know that Mason made a fuss at Mort's Partytime because all he wanted was the big glasses and not the full Buddy Holly outfit." He looked at Angie. "You know what put me onto the Mort's thing? I saw some of their bags in his room the day of the murder. Didn't think anything of it at the time, but later on it all started to add up. I believe Mason dressed up to look like Junior and wandered around the lake that afternoon so someone would see him."

Angie glared at Charlie, and for the first time he sensed some uncertainty in her manner.

"And here's something else," Charlie said. "Carmen was shot seven times. Five shots were sprayed all over his chest. A real pro would have plugged him in the heart a time or two and then maybe finished him with a head shot. It looks to me like the person who shot Carmen might have panicked. An amateur like Mason. I understand Mason isn't a total stranger to guns, though. Wasn't he arrested a couple of years ago for threatening someone outside a bar?"

Angie continued to glare at him, saying nothing.

"And here's the final point," he said. "Mason has no corroborated alibi for the afternoon Carmen was killed."

Suddenly Angie's smile returned, only there was no warmth in her eyes. "Oh, that's not true," she said. "He has a very good alibi."

"Really?" Charlie asked, trying to sound surprised. "What is it?"

"He was with me that afternoon."

Charlie had heard a lot of phony alibis, but none had ever sounded so sweet. "You told Walton that?" he asked, trying not to smile.

"Of course. What's the matter? Didn't your mother spend time with you?"

"Not much, to tell the truth," he said. "But I am surprised to hear you were with Mason."

"Oh, really. Where else would I have been?" She continued to flash her gotcha smile. "Come on Charlie. Enough questions. You can arrest Herbie and the cadaver in the morning and put an end to all of this."

Charlie walked to the bar, added some ice to his drink and slipped a hand in one pocket to click the off button on the small device. His insurance policy. "I'm really sorry you were with Mason that afternoon," he said.

Her smile faded again. "What's that supposed to mean?"

"Besides the other evidence, we have this." He handed her some photocopies he'd made at Kinko's.

She stared at them.

"These are blow-ups of frames from a surveillance video taken at Tony's Sporting Goods," Charlie said. "They show Mason purchasing .22 caliber ammunition just after noon on the day of the murder. See the time? And notice how he takes off his big glasses in this frame? No question that's Mason. Same clothes as the guy in your neighbor's photograph, too. And you know, as careful as Mason was in setting things up, he used his credit card to pay for the ammo. Guess he doesn't appreciate the value of cash."

Angie continued to stare blankly at the photocopies.

"It's not good, Angie. Looks like you're an accomplice."

She looked at him and laughed, a bit nervously Charlie thought. "That will never stand up," she said. "You know I was with you that afternoon."

"Really," he said slowly, furling his brows. "Now where was that?"

"The Frontage Motel." Concern was suddenly evident in her eyes. "What are you trying to do, you bastard?"

Charlie looked puzzled. "You didn't say anything to Kyle Walton about being with me," he said. "You're on the record as saying you were with Mason all afternoon. In fact, you just told me the same thing. And I don't think you'll find any record of me being at any motel that day. We've had a lot of burglaries around Springdale lately and I was real busy working those cases."

FLY LIKE A BIRD

There were days when Pete Thorsen missed his law practice. He remembered what it was like to sit across the conference table from opposing counsel and negotiate the terms of a deal with big bucks on the line. With his associates hovering by his side, he'd command the attention of everyone in the room as he floated a proposal to break an impasse over some major sticking point. He prided himself on being a dealmaker, and when he was finished, he could sense the gradual relief that spread through the room as the parties bought into his idea. Buoyed by their success in getting past a major hurdle, they seemed eager to compromise on other issues to get the deal done. For him, the greatest satisfaction came from knowing that the proposal gave his client exactly what it wanted all along without torpedoing the transaction.

At the closing, he would stalk around the conference room like a general surveying a battlefield, eyeing the final documents standing upright in ridiculously-long accordion-like folders. His lieutenants would be meticulously checking to make sure everything was in order. After the signing, it was time to break out the celebratory champagne — the good stuff — and toast each other for a job well done. Accolades would flow for the foresight of the businessmen in doing the deal and for the ingenuity and hard work of counsel in making it all happen.

He missed the camaraderie of his practice, too. He stared at the old Viking battle axe, a reminder of his heritage, that hung on his wall. At one time, before he gave up his spacious corner office in one of Chicago's glitzy office towers, the axe had occupied a prominent place over his credenza. He grinned when he thought of some of the jokes it had provoked. The best came from tart-tongued partner Angie DeMarco, invariably shoehorned into one of her tailored suits that disguised her tough-as-nails demeanor. She'd pop into his office after a contentious partners meeting and tell him how badly he'd handled things. Then she'd needle him mercilessly about having taken the axe to some vulnerable part of an obnoxious partner's anatomy. At the end, they'd share a good laugh.

The reasons he'd decided to pack it in swept over him like a flood. For starters, he just got sick of calibrating his life into six-minute billable hour segments for the Accounting Department. It was a little thing, and essential to the business side of any successful firm, but as the years passed, that didn't stop it from grating on him. Moving along the spectrum, once he became the firm's managing partner, there was the constant hassle of dealing with the growing cadre of younger partners who were predisposed to reduce everything to dollars and cents and seemed to care little about the century-old institution that he loved. Where were the lawyers he used to go to lunch with as a junior associate and talk about Cezanne or the latest historical work by David McCullough?

He stared at his computer screen and sighed. The fact was, he enjoyed his new freedom. He could sleep till seven, go for a run along Crystal Lake with the water glistening in the low morning sun like a million diamonds, take on only those legal matters that interested him, and dress the way he wanted when he went to his small office on Main Street. He liked his new life as an author, too, frustrating as it could be. Life was a series of tradeoffs, and he'd made his.

He turned back to the note cards that covered his desk. He'd always wanted to write a series of essays about the lake and now he had the time. He stared at the cards, occasionally moving them around like pieces of a jig saw puzzle. He didn't believe in writer's block, but was going through a period when nothing seemed to flow. It had been that way for the past week. On any other day, he would have put his work aside and walked down the street to the offices of *The Northern Sentinel* to kibitz with his friend, Harry McTigue, but even that option wasn't available to him. Harry was off at another one of his newspaper conferences and wouldn't be back for two more days.

As he sat there, idly tapping his pen on his desk, he heard his outer door open. The soft sound of rolling wheels followed, like the UPS man had just arrived and was pushing a loaded dolly across the floor. That's funny, he thought. He didn't remember ordering anything. He rose from his chair to check. A young man he didn't recognize had maneuvered a wheel chair through the outer door and was pushing it toward his office.

"Robyn," he said when he saw the woman in the chair. "I thought you'd gone back to Harbor Springs."

"Hello, Peter. No, I'm still here." Robyn Fleming was the only person he knew — his late mother excepted — who called him by his full first name. She was in her forties with streaks of gray running through hair that was pulled back into a functional pony tail. Not a perky style with hair sticking out of a pink cap, but a simple 'do that served only to keep her hair away from her face. As usual, her face was free of makeup.

Below the neck, though, Robyn looked like a peacock. She wore a bight yellow dress that concealed the extra pounds that came with being confined to a wheel chair for seven years. Her feet were decked out in a pair of blue athletic shoes with lightning bolts on the sides. The contrast always intrigued him. Maybe those who traced her frumpy hair and lack of makeup to her accident were right.

"You look busy," Robyn said, eyeing the top of his desk. "I can come back later."

"No, no, please stay," Pete replied. "I was just sitting here daydreaming, anyway."

A faint smile creased her face. "Daydreaming," she mused. "About the days when Pete Thorsen used to be an important lawyer?"

He was always amazed, and found it a little spooky, that Robyn could read his mind so well and seemingly detect his innermost thoughts. He must be an open book. Or maybe she'd acquired mystical powers to compensate for what she'd lost in her legs.

"Oh, sure, Robyn," he replied with false sarcasm. "I miss being the corner fire hydrant for every Doberman wannabe in Chicago."

Robyn smiled again and turned to her caregiver. "Tom," she said, "I have to talk to Peter about some things. Could you leave us alone for a while? I'll call you on your cell phone when I'm ready to leave."

After he'd left, she wheeled her chair closer to Pete's desk and said, "You do look more relaxed than you used to, counselor."

He grinned at her. "That's what living at the lake and writing a book will do for you."

"And fishing and playing golf, too, Harry tells me."

He grinned again. "It's a tough life, but as they say, someone's got to do it."

"I'm beginning to understand what you like about golf," she said, pointing to some watercolors of golf courses that hung on his wall. "I tried it a couple of times when I still had use of my legs. I didn't care for it in those days; not enough excitement. Now I understand it has a different kind of excitement. Maybe I'll try it again. I hear they have wheel chair golf."

"You should," he replied. "It's a cerebral sport. A lot of inner satisfaction. Peaceful, too, if you have the right companions." And a lot less dangerous than hang gliding, he thought to himself.

Robyn looked pensive for a moment. Then she said, "I know most people wouldn't compare the two, but hang gliding is peaceful, too. The solitude you feel when you soar above the earth. No engine noise in your ears. Nothing but peace. That's what birds must experience every day."

That was an interesting way to put it, he thought. Then he asked delicately, "Do you know how Sean is doing?"

Robyn looked down. "I was in Tràverse City last night," she said. "They're going to move him to a hospital in Ann Arbor."

"Has there been any improvement in his condition?"

She bit her lower lip and looked as though she were about to cry. "Too early to tell," she replied. "We'll know better in a week. They're planning more surgery, I'm told."

Sean O'Toole was involved in an accident at a hang gliding event in Elberta over the weekend. One minute he was soaring above the Lake Michigan beach and the next he was plummeting to earth in a tangle of flesh and aluminum alloy. His wing was folded over like a wounded duck.

Robyn dabbed at her eyes. Then she looked at Pete and said, "It was awful," and began to cry.

Pete knew the trauma she must be experiencing as a result of Sean's accident. When it looked like she'd regained her composure, he asked as gently as he could "Do they know what happened?"

"No," she said, her voice taking on an edge. "They seem more concerned with that than with Sean's recovery." She wiped her eyes again. "I heard a Deputy say it could have been material fatigue or maybe the wing was damaged in some way and Sean didn't notice it before he launched."

His friend Harry had told him the same thing. He'd been on the Elberta beach the morning Sean O'Toole went down, covering the hang gliding event for his paper. He said that by the time the crowd below realized something was wrong, Sean was in a downward spiral, heading right for a pile of rocks and scrub brush. He seemed to pick up speed as he fell, landing with a sickening thud.

The irony was that seven years earlier, while participating in a hang gliding event in Pennsylvania, Robyn had been involved in a similar accident. She'd never regained use of her legs despite several operations and extensive therapy. For two months, she barely spoke to anyone, but then she seemed to come around and gradually put the pieces of her life back together.

"I was on the beach watching, you know," Robyn continued softly. "Sean and his new partner were doing aerobatics for the crowd. Simple loops and that kind of thing. He had on his favorite suit," she said. "Blue with yellow lightning bolts." She looked at her shoes and tears welled up in her eyes again. "He looked so graceful up there. I wish I could have been with him."

She brushed away a tear. "Then he started to fall to earth," she continued.

Pete said nothing and waited for her to continue.

"It took so long for him to come down," she said wistfully. "I know it was only a short while, but for someone who's been a hang glider, he looked like he was frozen in time."

"Didn't he have a chute or didn't it open or what?"

Robyn looked at him with a steady gaze. "Sean never carried a chute. He felt it weighed him down. Even when the rules of an event required chutes, Sean found a way around it. Carried an empty pack, that sort of thing." She brushed at her eyes again. "I think it also heightened his sense of excitement to be up there without safety equipment."

Pete thought that was suicidal, but again said nothing. He wondered what Sean O'Toole would give now to have had a chute to ease him down.

"I loved hang gliding," Robyn said wistfully. "You fly like a bird. Sean was the best." She started to cry again.

"I miss it so. Have you ever had to give up something you loved?"

Pete thought about her question. How ironic she'd ask a question like that on a day when he was having second thoughts about having given up his law practice. It wasn't the same, he knew, but giving up something he'd worked all his life for gave him some idea of the point she was making. Still, he couldn't imagine what it would be like to give up something he loved because he was physically unable to do it anymore. "Robyn," he said gently, "we've been through this before. Why beat yourself up? Sean knew the risks of what he was doing."

Robyn's lips tightened and her expression suddenly looked fierce. "That sounds so cold, Peter. You've never tried it, have you?"

"No," he said gently, "I've never tried it." Nor had he been tempted. He thought back to his army days when he spent two weeks in jump school and remembered the anxiety he felt every time he stood atop the training tower. Finally, he dropped out. He never told anyone of the real reason, but rather deflected the issue by telling people, in a self-deprecating way, that he was enthusiastic about the airborne until he discovered you had to jump out of airplanes. If jump school made him queasy, he could only imagine what hang gliding without a chute would do.

"People are always so quick to judge," she continued heatedly. "They love to watch someone like Sean, but if something goes wrong, they're quick to condemn hang gliding or the fact he didn't have a chute."

He'd gotten used to Robyn's emotional outbursts over the years. He tried to treat her with kid gloves, but every now and then, he said something that set her off. At one time, Robyn and Sean were inseparable. They'd go from hang glide festival to hang glide festival, from launch site to launch site, soaring through the sky like twin birds in their matching jump suits. They reminded him of two skydivers he'd once seen when he was at the University of Wisconsin. One Sunday afternoon in February, when the air was crisp and the sky a perfect cobalt-blue, they dove onto frozen Lake Mendota trailing flares that emitted orange smoke. When they landed, they disappeared behind a snow barricade on the lake. When they didn't appear, the crowd on shore became fearful that they'd broken through the ice. All of a sudden, after five minutes, the skydivers leaped into view of the anxious spectators in a dramatic moment. Everyone stood speechless initially, then broke into frenzied applause. It was a moment that the divers seemed to enjoy as much as the crowd.

Robyn and Sean shared a similar flare for the theatrical. Everyone in the hang gliding world knew them. They were a pair, soaring above the earth like two graceful peacocks. Then Robyn's accident happened and it cast a pall over the sport. She was lucky, though. She eventually regained use of her arms, but remained paralyzed from the waist down.

Pete first met Robyn when she was rehabbing. She'd only gone to college for one year, but his late wife, Doris, had been her roommate. Doris and Robyn had drifted apart after Robyn dropped out of school, but Doris heard about her accident and reestablished contact. Partly at Doris' urging, Robyn, who was originally from Grand Rapids, moved to Harbor Springs where she bought a small antiques shop and worked at trying to get her life back. Through Doris' good offices, Pete wound up representing her and her new business. Robyn didn't fit the firm's *pro bono* profile but he pulled some strings so he could represent her without charge. She'd been a client ever since.

Pete had the unpleasant experience of observing first-hand the slow disintegration of a relationship in which the lives of two people diverged — one partner healthy and wanting to continue with his lifestyle, the other disabled and having special needs. At first, Sean made regular visits to Harbor Springs to see Robyn. Then he got an endorsement deal with a manufacturer of hang glide equipment and his trips became fewer. Robyn made excuses for him when he cancelled scheduled visits. Then, by pure happenstance, Doris picked up information that Sean had a "new" Robyn. Barely 20 years old, the young lady became Sean's regular companion in the hang gliding world and the visits to Harbor Springs stopped altogether.

When news got out that a reunion was planned for Elberta to celebrate the old hang gliding days, Sean's name became associated with the event even though he was too young to have been a participant during the hey days of the 1970s. By that time, Robyn had heard about Sean's new partner, but put up a brave face. She had to be hurting, but she made plans to be at the launch site. In a poignant gesture, she even had a special jump suit made for her to match the one she used to wear with Sean. Then Sean's accident happened on the first day of the reunion event.

Pete wasn't quite sure what to say in light of Robyn's latest outburst. "I'm sorry, Robyn. I was just talking without thinking."

"No, Peter, I'm the one who should apologize. There was no reason for me to treat you that way."

They sat quietly for a few minutes. Then Pete said, "When you came in, you said there was something you wanted to talk about." He looked at her and waited for her to respond.

Robyn continued to look at the floor. "Are you my lawyer, Peter?"

He was puzzled by her question and not sure what she was getting at, but said, "Of course, Robyn. I've been your lawyer for years."

"I was just wondering," she said. "You've never charged me a fee or anything."

"No," he said. "I've never charged you a fee because I've represented you *pro bono*. But *pro bono* clients are still clients. Why are you asking now, after all these years, Robyn?"

"Just wondering," she said. "Could I ask you one more question before I tell you what's on my mind?"

"Sure," he replied.

"I remember you once telling me that a lawyer has a duty of confidentiality to his clients. For example, if I tell my lawyer — you — something in confidence, you can't repeat what I said to anyone else."

"That's essentially true. There are some exceptions, but generally speaking, I have to keep what you tell me confidential."

She sat there quietly for a few moments. He waited patiently for her to speak.

"I'm thinking of bringing Sean into my business when he recovers," she finally said. "I wanted to talk to you about it, but wanted to be sure there was no misunderstanding as to confidence just in case I change my mind."

He wasn't expecting that. Robyn had built her antiques business into the most successful one in Harbor Springs with an enviable list of wealthy customers. It was a terrible time to talk about bringing an old boyfriend into the business. But he knew if he gave her his honest advice, he risked setting her off again. "We could talk about alternatives, Robyn," he finally said. When she didn't reply, he added, "You could have Sean work with you without actually bringing him into the business, you know. Make him second in command, or something."

"I realize that," she said, staring at the floor again, "but let's say I wanted to bring Sean into an ownership position. How would I do it?"

Pete hadn't represented many small businesses, but he was aware of all the horror stories. Enough things could go wrong in a business relationship without the personal trauma of dual disabilities hanging over the partners' heads. Maybe with time, she would see the wisdom of going slowly. In spite of his misgivings, he took 15 minutes and explained the various organizational structures for small business and the advisability of buy-sell agreements even for those that were owned by family members or close personal friends. After that, they spent time talking about how those things would work if Sean were to be brought into her antiques business. Pete made her promise to think about it for a while before she made her final decision or said anything to Sean.

"One more question, Peter."

Pete nodded and sat back while she collected her thoughts. "You don't do criminal work, do you?"

"No," he said slowly, "I'm a corporate lawyer. Criminal is a whole separate field."

Robyn bit her lower lip again and didn't meet his eyes. "When they finish examining Sean's wing, I may need a criminal lawyer, Peter."

Pete got a sick feeling in the pit of his stomach when he realized what she was saying. He searched for the right words, and finally said, "But you're confined to a wheelchair, Robyn. How would you...?"

She interrupted him. "I know this man in Traverse City, Peter."

He couldn't speak for a full minute. Then he said weakly, "Why, Robyn?"

Her eyes were glistening again and tears rolled down her cheeks. "I didn't mean for Sean to get hurt that bad," she said between sobs. "I thought that if his legs were hurt like mine, we'd have a common bond to be together again."

DOMINIC'S ART

When I hung out my shingle as "Nilsen Investigations," I wasn't foolish enough to expect a stacked blonde to stroll into my office on the first day, plunk down a wad of c-notes, and hire me to find some fabled jewel-encrusted statue. At the same time, I'd promised myself I wouldn't work the bottom end of the food chain just to make a buck. Meaning domestic surveillance cases. The kind where one spouse wants the goods on the other, backed by nine-by-twelve glossies.

But after two months in business, my resolve was being tested. The landlord was hounding me for the next month's rent, my latest phone bill had just arrived and the only opportunities in sight were three of the pooh cases I'd vowed to avoid.

Then Birley Girnwood showed up in my South Wabash office, clutching one of the flyers I'd been circulating in select circles to get the word out about my talents. He plopped into one of my molded plastic guest chairs and appeared to give me the once over with close-set dark eyes. With his hawkish features, hunched shoulders and bony frame, he reminded me of some outsized bird of prey.

Birley also owned Girnwood Galleries, located in Chicago's tony Gold Coast. He told me he was convinced that his junior partner, John Huber, had been stealing from him and wanted me to investigate. Junior partner was a misnomer he quickly added in his *faux* English accent; Huber was really just an employee.

Titles aside, with the prospect of a real case, my eyes lit up like one of the slots on a riverboat casino. After letting Birley ramble on for five minutes, I decided I'd shown enough cool. I grabbed his retainer check and hustled it down to my bank before he could say "Whistler's Mother."

The following morning, fortified with a jumbo cup of coffee from Kyros Diner next door, I began to scour the records Birley had left for signs of wrongdoing. I tackled the financial ledgers first. After three hours, the only conclusion I was able to reach was that double-entry bookkeeping, the accepted standard everywhere, was not widely practiced at Girnwood Galleries. I moved on to the art inventory records and found they consisted mostly of scraps of paper with a few scribbles, typically in Huber's barely legible hand.

"Have you discovered anything, Mr. Nilsen?" Birley asked after he'd popped into my office unannounced late that afternoon. "By the way, do you mind if I call you Halvor?"

That is my name, Halvor Nilsen. Scandinavian to the bone in a profession that seemed to be dominated by the Irish and Italians. "Hal will do just fine," I said, donning my everyman hat. "But to answer your question, no, I haven't found anything yet."

Birley flicked at his gray tweed suit a couple of times and studied his buffed fingernails. "I'm sure something is going on," he said, looking at me with his sharp eyes. "Our cash is low and we seem to be missing a few pieces of art. I'm convinced Mr. Huber is behind it all."

"Possible," I said. "But I can't tell just from your records. If you don't mind me saying, they're a bit of a mess."

He waved one hand. "I know, I know," he said. "It's just that I'm totally into art. That's what makes me vulnerable. But I expect you'll be able to come up with the proof we need, Hal. Mind you, I would prefer to handle this confidentially with Mr. Huber and not take it to the authorities if I can avoid doing so."

After he left, I propped my feet on the gunmetal gray desk I'd inherited from the previous tenant, tried to ignore the peeling paint on my ceiling, and did what every good detective is supposed to do — cogitate. An epiphany didn't reveal itself, but my decision to have a first-hand look at Girnwood Galleries was a start.

■ ■ ■

The next day, after catching up on some paperwork, which consisted mostly of sorting through a handful of flyers that had been slipped under my door, I grabbed a bowl of soup and some baklava at Kyros and then took a cab north to visit Birley.

Girnwood Galleries is on Oak Street, a block west of Michigan Avenue. One glance told me the gallery was doing its part to uphold neighborhood standards. Pricey-looking oils that could have been painted by the Old Masters filled the walls; there wasn't a poster or print in sight. Birley hovered at the far end next to a dowager with, I swear, blue hair. Her eyes were glued to a landscape painted in soothing autumnal colors.

When Birley spotted me, he frowned and was at my side in two bounds of his whippet-like body.

"Hal," he said in a barely audible but irritated croak, "you didn't tell me you were coming over."

"I thought I should have a look at the scene of the crime, so to speak," I said, sweeping the room with my eyes. "Very impressive."

"I can't talk now," Birley whispered hoarsely. His eyes darted about as though he were fearful of being seen with me. "We're very busy today."

"No problem," I said. "I'll just look around and then take my leave."

"Okay," he whispered again, "but don't call attention to yourself. And don't bother any of my customers."

I moved slowly around the gallery, trying to look like a man with a keen appreciation for the visual arts. Then I saw him. Dominic Ambrosi. The mug shots I'd seen back in the days when I worked homicide for the Chicago PD didn't do him justice. His gray suit matched his slicked-back hair and screamed two thousand bucks. The guys flanking him were straight from central casting for *The Sopranos*.

Birley saw him at the same time I did and was at his side before I could hum a few bars from my favorite *Goodfellas* movie. Ambrosi stood in front of a portrait of a regal woman who wore a simple blue dress with a scooped neckline that displayed just a hint of cleavage. She had wide-set oval eyes, a long straight nose and a heart-shaped mouth. Her dark hair trailed down her back in soft ringlets. With my keen eye for these things, I wondered how I'd missed the piece.

Birley whispered in Ambrosi's ear and pointed at the painting. Ambrosi nodded, but like a man who was only half listening. After more whispers and gestures, Birley touched Ambrosi's sleeve, raised an index finger and skittered back toward blue hair. Ambrosi's eyes never left the painting.

I tapped Birley's arm as he passed. "Isn't that Dominic Ambrosi?" I asked.

His eyebrows inched up his pasty forehead. "Yes, that's Mr. Ambrosi. Do you know him?"

"Only by reputation from my old job. He's connected as I recall."

Birley's eyes betrayed his anxiety. "Would Mr. Ambrosi recognize you?"

I shrugged. "Unlikely, but I suppose it's possible."

"Hurry," Birley said, hastily nudging me through a drapery-covered doorway, "go in back. I'll let you know when he's gone."

Safely sequestered, I looked around the room. It was a jumble of frames, blank canvasses and packing crates. Paintings of various sizes rested against the walls, many draped with protective coverings. I took a look at a few of them. One, a portrait of a lady in a blue dress, caught my eye, possibly because it was so similar to the piece Dominic Ambrosi had been eyeing so intently. Maybe the same artist, I thought. Possibly a companion portrait.

I was flipping through some art and antiques publications when Birley stuck his head through the curtain, looking more relaxed, and gave the all-clear sign. "I'll call you in the morning," he said.

"Did he buy it?" I asked.

Birley looked back and his lips curled into as much of a smile as I'd seen from him. "He has it on hold."

When I reentered the main gallery, he was writing a sales slip for blue hair and wore the expression of a man who'd had a good day.

■ ■ ■

My phone was ringing when I opened my office door the next morning. It was Birley. He took me to task for showing up at the gallery without checking with him first, and then pumped me about whether I'd spotted anything useful during my visit. Nothing that would incriminate John Huber, I said. Then I added a gratuitous quip about not knowing he was an art purveyor to the mob. He didn't seem amused.

That night, I staked out Huber's apartment in a building just off West Randolph. One of the reasons I'd gotten out of police work was that I hated stakeouts. But there I was, at it again, and in February no less.

Huber finally showed about nine, just when the temperature inside my old Chevy had reached frostbite levels. I slid out of the car as quietly as I could and moved up behind him as he fumbled with his keys.

"John Huber?" I asked.

Huber jerked upright like he'd been jabbed in the back. The keys dropped from his hand and clattered on the concrete steps. His eyes were wide when he turned and saw me standing five feet away. "What do you want?" he asked. There was a tremor in his voice.

"I'm Hal Nilsen. A private investigator. I'd like to ask you a few questions."

He blinked a few times. "About what?"

"Oh, missing artwork, pilfered cash, things like that. I work for Girnwood Galleries."

He looked at me for a moment and seemed on the verge of regaining his composure. "Birley hired you?"

"That's right."

"That's ridiculous," he said disdainfully. "I have nothing to say to you." He folded his arms across his chest.

There are a few things I can't tolerate, and one is to be jerked around by a guy I'm trying to engage in a reasonable conversation. Something about John Huber's manner suggested he might need a little extra incentive to reciprocate my reasonableness. I unzipped my jacket and let it fall open to expose the Glock.

"We need to talk," I said, squinting at him in the dim light. "Inside."

Fear returned to Huber's eyes at the sight of the piece. "You're not going to hurt me, are you?" The tremor in his voice was back. "I didn't do anything."

"I just want to talk to you, John."

Huber hesitated for a moment and then picked up his keys. He fumbled with the lock, hands shaking, while I waited as patiently as I could, freezing my butt off. He managed to get the door open just as I was about to grab the keys and do it myself.

Huber's apartment was a large open loft with a living area in one corner. The rest of the space was cluttered with easels, paintings and art supplies.

"I didn't know you were an artist," I said. He just scowled.

Most of Huber's paintings were abstracts in depressing shades of black and gray. But two pieces on adjacent easels stood out. One was a small oil painting of a traditional landscape. The other, as best I could tell, was identical. I stared at the pieces for a few moments and then shifted my gaze back toward Huber.

The scowl was still there but his hands gave him away. Finally, seeming uncomfortable with the silence, he said, "There's nothing wrong with practicing brush technique by studying another piece."

I continued to stare at him and said nothing. Images from my visit to Girnwood Galleries flashed through my mind.

"I've had enough of this!" Huber said, exhibiting another mood change. "Get out or I'll call the police." He walked toward the phone, face flushed, and jabbed a finger in my direction. "And I'm going to press charges against you for threatening me with a gun."

I'd learned long ago that if you were going to threaten a man, it was best to do it when your hands weren't trembling like aspen leaves in a stiff breeze. Huber obviously lacked the same life experience.

"First of all," I said, "I'm licensed to carry this gun and I never threatened you. But go ahead and call. I'll be curious to see how you explain your interesting art studies. And the missing cash at the gallery."

Huber's mouth opened as though he were going to reply. Then his shoulders slumped and he dropped into an old wing chair that looked like it had come from the Salvation Army reject pile. I took a seat on a couch that was even less upscale and waited for him to collect himself. After staring into space for a while, Huber opened up and bared his soul. Then he sat back, moist-eyed, and pleaded his case. Maybe he was a slime ball, but my softer side took over and I offered some personal thoughts on redemption, just for what they might be worth.

■ ■ ■

Being played always upsets me and I decided to get away before I did something stupid. Birley hadn't been pleased when I told him I was going to Myrtle Beach for a week to look in on a sick aunt. And he'd become nearly apoplectic when I said I needed another check to replenish his retainer. His mood did seem to improve a bit when I told him I thought the investigation could be wrapped up shortly after my return.

Myrtle Beach was just the tonic I needed. I never did manage to locate that aunt, but met a woman who played a nice game of golf. She even helped me lower my own scores by a few strokes. Maybe it had something to do with her talent for working the kinks out of my body after each round. Her sommelier's knowledge of Oregon pinot noirs was a real plus, too.

My first morning back in the office, I checked in with John Huber. He assured me he'd followed through on his vow, which made me feel a little better about human nature. Then I began work on my report to Birley. I finished the following day and dressed the report up in a nice cover I'd purchased from OfficeMax. It was my first case, and I wanted things to look professional. I made the obligatory stop at Kyros and then headed for Girnwood Galleries.

It was after hours and Birley was waiting to let me in. He seemed more interested in my report than social pleasantries, so I plunged right in and told him that John Huber had admitted to borrowing cash a few times and to occasionally taking home a painting or two. Birley seemed pleased to hear of the confession, but when I added that Huber claimed Birley knew about everything in advance, his noggin began to shake like a bobble-head doll with a serious malfunction.

"Not true, Hal, not true. I've had my suspicions, as you're aware. But if I'd known exactly what Mr. Huber was doing, why would I have hired you?"

I resisted the temptation to answer and watched as Birley walked over to a desk and unlocked a drawer. "Look," he said, returning with a log book. "Everyone who takes art from the gallery, if it's not a firm sale, must sign for it. Even me." He pointed to his signature in several places. "This is one area where we do keep good records, Hal. Do you see Mr. Huber's signature anywhere? And no one can take a cash advance without my approval and giving the company a note."

I scanned the log but didn't see Huber's signature. "Well, it's all in here," I said, tapping my report. "If I were you, I'd take this to the States Attorney's office and see if they'll prosecute."

Birley raised his hand. "No, Hal, people make mistakes. I'm sure I can work things out with Mr. Huber now that the facts are known."

I nodded. "It's up to you, of course." Then I pointed to where the portrait of the woman had hung. "You must have closed the sale to Mr. Ambrosi."

His lips curled into that half smile again. "Yes," he said, "I had to give him a nice discount, but it was still a six-figure sale."

I whistled. "He must have really liked it."

"Very much," he said, "but it is a very fine piece by a prominent American portrait artist of Italian descent." Then he added with another little curl of his lips, "And of course it didn't hurt that the lady in the painting looked like his maternal grandmother when she was younger."

I winked at him. "You're the best. By the way, just between us, which painting did you sell him?"

His eyebrows rose. "What do you mean? I sold him the portrait. Lady in Blue."

"Yes, I know," I said. "But which one? The piece that was hanging on the wall or the one you've been storing in back?"

Birley's eyes narrowed. "I don't follow you, Hal."

"Sure you do," I said. "John Huber has quite an operation in his loft. He takes art home with your approval, produces copies and you sell them in your gallery, or sometimes in galleries you're affiliated with around the country if it seems too risky to do it here in Chicago."

"That's absurd," Birley said with a sniff. "I have no idea what Mr. Huber does in his loft, but it has nothing to do with me. A man like that will do or say anything."

"I can't attest as to Huber's character," I said, "but I did see a duplicate of Lady in Blue in your back room when you shooed me out of sight that day. Is it still there?"

Birley's mouth twitched. "Your baseless allegations are becoming very offensive, Mr. Nilsen. And that aside, do you really believe I'd be foolish enough to sell forged art to a man like Mr. Ambrosi? Besides, he had the piece vetted before he purchased it."

"Ahhh. Then I assume he took the painting with him immediately after it was vetted."

"Of course not," Birley said, plainly disgusted with my ignorance. "We always carefully pack valuable works of art so they won't be damaged in transit. That's one thing Mr. Huber is very good at."

"So the fake could have been packed up and delivered to Mr. Ambrosi." I shook my head. "I'd check if I were you." Birley's eyes instinctively flicked toward the back room, but he didn't take my bait and have a look-see. I knew he would later on, though, and would have given part of my fee just to watch the expression on his face as he searched madly for the other Lady in Blue.

"I think it's time for you to leave, Mr. Nilsen."

"Okay," I said, rising to my feet, "here's my report. Everything is in there. I don't think you'll find it much use to coerce John Huber into continuing with your forged art scheme, though. That's why you really hired me, isn't it? To pressure Huber because he wanted to quit?"

I watched Birley flip through the report, fumbling with the pages, and then added, "I also understand a local gossip columnist is onto a story about some Chicago gallery selling forged art." Birley's head snapped up and it looked as though he were about to cry.

The cold air felt good for a change. I spotted a mailbox, and after fingering the envelope in my pocket for a moment, slid it into the slot. When I reached Michigan Avenue, I walked south, lost in thought. I wondered whether Dominic Ambrosi was the kind of man who liked to receive mail. And if John Huber had packed the right piece. Then memories of my week at Myrtle Beach crowded out all other thoughts.

THE NIGHT THEY
CLOSED BAKER'S BAR

The first time I was in Baker's Bar, I was sitting at a table just inside the front door with my wife of seven months enjoying a couple of cold ones on a sultry summer night. Two Harley guys were lingering outside the place when we came in. They were bouncing up and down on their bikes and revving their engines. I figured them for a couple of rowdies trying to build reputations as the sons of Satan or something. Finally, they apparently lost what little restraint governed their twisted psyches, jumped the curb, and eased their machines through the door into the crowded barroom.

The roar of engines instantly drowned out the din of elbow-to-elbow revelers and exhaust fumes overpowered the stench of stale beer and cigarettes. Bodies near the door scrambled to get out of the way. Two guys in black muscle shirts holding court at the bar apparently decided they'd be the saviors of everyone else and jumped the bikers. They all went down in a tangle of flesh and metal. Acquaintances of the bikers jumped into the fray on their side and the melee was on. Chairs flew and fists pounded into human flesh and angry voices could be heard above the chug of the idling Harleys flopped on the floor.

Now I've been in a serious fight exactly once — in a bar in Stanley, Idaho, the jumping off point for float trips down the Middle Fork of the Salmon River, when some river rats provoked a bunch of militia-types by calling them "misfits" — and it taught me one of life's enduring lessons: chairs don't shatter when they slam into a man's back, like they do in the old Western movies, but rather leave you paralyzed and fearing you'll never walk again. And if wood does that, you can only imagine what tubular steel does.

My highly-developed instincts for survival took over as soon as the fight began. Through the tangled mass of bodies and machines, I spotted a table with no one cowering beneath it. I scrambled madly for safety and reached the table with little more than a kick or two in the ribs. There I lay like a whipped puppy seeking shelter from a brutal master, thinking of no one or nothing except my personal safety.

In due course, the cops arrived and restored order. When I was satisfied that chairs had ceased flying, I cautiously hoisted myself to my feet and examined my body for damaged parts. Thankfully, I found none. One of the self-appointed saviors in the black muscle shirt wasn't so lucky, though. My last glimpse of him was when they carried his body out on a stretcher with blood dripping from a huge gash on the side of his head.

Years later, long after my marriage had ceased bumping along the bottom and had finally hit the Big Snag, I was in Baker's Bar again. The legendary watering hole was going mainstream and it was the last night before the joint ceased being a pure bar and morphed into a place that emphasized food and catered to the mobs of tourists who walked aimlessly up and down Main Street in July and August. Now the big deal would be getting a table for the Friday night fish fry rather than gaining entrance to rub elbows with the bikers and assorted other rowdies. The place even planned to change its name, I was told. Henceforth it would be Dinghy's, or something like that.

As I think back, I often reflect on how that first night at Baker's changed my life. Now I'm not blaming the bar for the demise of my marriage or anything like that. There were a lot of other factors, too. But when I spotted my ex picking herself up off the floor that night, her hair drenched with beer and a lump on her head the size of a prize turnip and blood trickling from her nose, I somehow knew it was the beginning of the end.

Six months later, she began wearing jeans that looked like they'd been painted on and started going out with her girlfriends two or three nights a week. On some of the other nights, when she thought I was asleep, she'd sneak out for more good times. Gordon Lightfoot's old hit song, "Sundown," had some good advice about what to do when a man finds that his woman is sneaking down the back stairs, but I didn't have the gumption to follow it. Thought things would just get better, I guess.

I was also convinced it wasn't my fault that my self-preservation instincts took over that night and squeezed out all other emotions. Those were instincts developed to cope with a hostile world in which danger lurked like a three-headed monster. I suppose I could have manned-up and dragged my ex under that table with me. And before that, I could have started wearing black muscle shirts once in a while, like those guys at the bar, instead of my standard pique shirts with matching trim on the sleeves and cute little golf man logos on the front. Maybe even started drinking my beer from a bottle rather than always asking for a glass. But all of that is hindsight, and I doubt it would have overcome basic instincts when push came to shove.

On that last night in Baker's, the place was teeming with nostalgic drinkers and I was damned lucky to find a seat at the bar, toward the end, under the sign that read, "Ann Arbor No. 7" to commemorate the old car ferry days. I'm not much of a beer drinker anyway, and after sitting there for a while with my hands wrapped around the bottle, my Amstel Light was beginning to taste like fresh pee from one of those funny looking animals that live on that farm over on River Road.

It was hot in Baker's, too, and I was beginning to feel a bit uncomfortable. I'd bought a black muscle shirt for the occasion and laundered it three times to get some of the newness out. But I could have laundered it every day for a month straight and it wouldn't have softened the part with a devilish-looking rock star stenciled on it. I resisted the temptation to start scratching madly where the rock guy was tormenting my skin. My golf shirts never itched like that, I thought petulantly.

My peripheral vision has always been good, and as I sat there with elbows on the bar and doing everything I could to look like a stud, I noticed this babe with raven black hair and tight black jeans like my ex used to wear. She was making her way through the crowd to the juke box again. I wasn't keeping track or anything, but noted she'd already played that old country favorite, "Elvira," at least six times. Now I like that song, too, but six times in a row? C'mon, lady, give the crowd a break. Jeez! I had no idea what the woman's name was, but dubbed her Elvira. Somehow it fit her, too, because I'd always envisioned the woman in that song with black hair and dressed all in black. Intriguing as she was, I made a conscious decision to block her out and resumed thinking about my life.

Pretty soon I feel these warm, soft boobies pressing against my back, and I think, holy shit, my ex is back! But when I swiveled my head to look, I saw that it was Elvira. She was pressing her body so close to mine that I was sure she'd leave creases in my shirt. Her perfume was strong, too, and almost made my eyes water.

"You look like you could use a friend," she said.

"Just sitting here thinking, Elvira." I knew it was a mistake the moment the words came out of my mouth. I hadn't meant to call her Elvira; it just slipped out. I could see her body stiffen and a wary look appear on her face as soon as I said it.

She said, "Do I know you?" The smile that was on her face when she first came up had vanished.

"I don't think so," I replied, trying to be jocular about it.

"You called me Elvira," she said.

"Yeah, I'm sorry, I didn't mean to."

Her dark eyes searched my face for a long time. "You're not one of those psychics, are you?"

I couldn't tell whether she was kidding or what. I forced a chuckle and said, "No, not me."

"Then why did you call me Elvira if you don't know me?"

I was beginning to feel a little uncomfortable with the conversation. I looked at her eyes again. Still no hint of a smile. Distraction, maybe or detachment. Obviously, I had upset her and scrambled for an explanation. "I just noticed you like that song," I said. "The name Elvira just slipped out. I don't know, subliminal or something."

She looked slightly more relieved and said, "You don't look like a psychic."

"Like I told you, I'm not. But I'm curious, what does a psychic look like?"

Her eyes darted around. "I don't know, kind of ishy."

"Ishy?"

"You know, strange. Kind of otherworldly. "

"I see."

"You can never tell about people, though," she said. "There are a lot more psychics out there than any of us wants to believe. Some of them don't even look like psychics. I met a guy once. He looked like a lawyer or accountant, but he was one of those psychics. I swear, that man could foretell everything."

"Like what?"

She looked at me with eyes that gave me the shudders just for a moment. "Like what was going to happen to my marriage, to give you an example."

"What did happen?"

"You mean with my marriage?"

"Yeah."

"My husband died." I looked at her eyes again; they didn't exactly look sorrowful. I thought about that, but quickly put it out of my mind. Maybe it was just one of those bad marriages. I was lucky. I didn't hate my ex-wife, much as I had cause to. I took a course once, and learned it wasn't healthy to hate.

I nodded at her response and then asked, "What did he die from?"

She lowered her voice and her reply really gave me the chills. "I think he was killed."

"In some kind of accident?" I asked.

Elvira looked at me with a mystical gleam in her eyes. "Don't know."

"You must have some idea of what happened," I said.

"Doctor said it might have been a heart attack, but I'm wondering whether that psychic had something to do with it."

I'm sure I had a startled expression on my face. "You mean he slipped your husband something that killed him? Made it look like a heart attack or something?" I read a mystery one time where the killer tried to disguise a murder that way.

"Could be," she replied. "Or put a spell on him or something. He acted awfully strange."

"He? You mean the psychic?"

"Yes."

"How did you meet this man? You were married, right?"

"Separated," she said and leaned closer, "I'd never cheat on my man." She gave a little shudder. "I don't want to talk about it anymore. When I came up, you said you were sitting here thinking. Thinking about what?"

"First, don't you think we should introduce ourselves? My name is David."

She hesitated a few moments and then a strange smile appeared on his face. "I'm Elvira," she said.

I suppressed my temptation to laugh. "You're kidding," I said.

"You act surprised."

"Oh, I'm not surprised. It's just that after our conversation and you playing that song over and over, I did envision Elvira with black hair and everything, and when you came up…oh hell, glad to meet you, Elvira."

"I feel relieved. So you're not one of those psychics after all."

"Nope, I'm not," I said, feeling relieved myself.

She gave me that coy smile again and took my hand. "I like you, David. Now you were telling me what you were thinking about."

I liked her, too, but couldn't quite squeeze out the words. Instead I said, "Oh, things. Reflecting on the old days at Baker's. Stuff like that."

"Were you a regular?"

"Not a regular," I said, "but I was in here a few times." I was stretching the truth a little, but what the hell, how would a woman like Elvira know that?

She ran a hand over my shoulder, and I tensed my bicep just before she got to my arm. I'd been going to the local health club and thought I'd seen some results. From the look in her eyes, she noticed, too. Truth is, I hate to work out, but if a woman like Elvira noticed, it was damn near worth it.

While I was thinking about it, Elvira moved her hand down and started feeling my ribs. I must have jumped a little or something, because she said, "Sorry."

"No problem," I said nonchalantly, "just ticklish I guess."

"I heard this used to be quite the place in the old days," Elvira said.

"If those signs could talk," I said with a sigh. "Ceiling, too," I went on, waving a hand at the car ferry signs that hung overhead.

"You like rough places?" she purred.

I shrugged and pressed my arm tighter against my side so the muscles stood out more. "It's part of the scene." I said. "I'm not the kind who goes looking for trouble; but sometimes it just finds you. I remember one time I was in here and these guys on Harleys came roaring in and threw the whole place up for grabs."

"What did you do?"

I shrugged again. "A fight broke out. A few of us tried to break it up. It got a little rough for a few minutes, though." I was getting into it now and I could tell Elvira was impressed.

"I like Harley guys. You ever ride a Harley?"

I shrugged a third time, like Harleys were tame stuff I did before breakfast, and was careful to keep my left arm squeezed against my side. "I've been on a bike or two."

"I bet you have," she said, rubbing a hand across my smooth-shaven face. "But you look so clean-cut. Was that in your past?"

I resisted the temptation to shrug a fourth time, thinking the expression of nonchalance would be too much. "You should have seen me in the days I was riding to Sturgis every year with ten thousand other bikers. Beard down to here," I said, making a gesture across my neck. "Hobnail boots, chain for a belt, the whole nine yards."

"Sturgis, is that the place out West where all the Harley guys go?"

"Guys with Harleys and a lot of other makes of bikes," I replied. I shook my head as though reflecting on the memories. "You should see the roads leading into Sturgis. Bikes as far as you can see."

"I'd like to see that sometime. Where do you keep your bike?"

My gut tightened. I'd backed my way into a corner with my big talk, but fortunately came up with a convenient explanation. "I sold my old bike a couple of weeks ago," I said. "Wanted something a little more powerful. I've been looking around for new equipment."

"I bet you miss it," she said. She ran her hand over my face again. "I like a man who's clean-shaven. Beards irritate my skin. That's the only thing I don't like about Harley guys."

I nodded knowingly. "That's why I cleaned myself up. I felt the beard and everything was me, but I was married to a woman just like you. Beards irritated her skin, too."

Elvira studied my face with hungry eyes. "Tell me about her. Did she have dark hair like mine?"

I kept my left arm pressed to my side, and reached over with my right hand and gave her hair a little toss. "Maybe a little lighter," I said. "Say, you want another drink?"

"Sure," she said. "Jack and water." She squeezed even closer to me and one of her boobs was flattened against my left arm. Her lips brushed my neck and sent tiny volts of electricity through my body. "You're so sensitive," she purred. "A lot of guys let a girl buy her own drinks all night and then want something later."

I swear, I was about to come unglued. This babe obviously had a big appetite, and of all the guys in Baker's, she'd singled me out for attention. "Common courtesy," I said nonchalantly. "And I don't expect anything," I added, suppressing the urge to shrug again. "If it happens, it happens."

She gave my arm a little squeeze. "You were telling me about your wife."

"Yeah, well, we just drifted apart. She wanted a white picket fence, three kids, a husband who comes home every night at six." I studied the bar for a few moments. "I guess my life was a little rough for her."

"Maybe she just wasn't woman enough to hold you."

This time I just couldn't resist the urge to shrug so I let one go. "Maybe," I said.

"A woman who's comfortable with herself knows when to hold a man close and when to give him some room." She was running her fingers over my ribs again and I tried not to flinch like I did the first time.

Christ, I was getting more worked up by the minute. She had a body that just wouldn't quit. Obviously, she understood men. I could only imagine what it would be like to tussle in the hay with her. She'd had a tragic life, that much seemed clear, but that only heightened her appeal. I deliberately shifted my position to rub against her boobs. She seemed to understand exactly what I was doing, gave me that sweet little smile again, and snuggled closer.

Elvira's lips brushed my ear. "We should go somewhere where it's not so crowded."

Man, it's not like I have a one-track mind or anything, but I was going crazy. I'd never been with a woman like her. What would I do after I got her alone? Reach over and feel her boob for starters? Then what? What if I'd misread her? "We could go for a walk down by the water," I said.

"I was thinking of something a little more private." She looked right at me while she wiggled her boobs back and forth against my arm. "Don't you have a place of your own?"

"Oh, sure," I said. "I've got a place. It's just temporary, though, until I find a bigger one." My mind was racing like Kurt Busch behind the wheel at Daytona. I wish I had cleaned up that damned place before I went out.

"Hey, David," a voice boomed over the din of the crowd, "what the hell you doing in here?"

I looked around and spotted my neighbor, Mikey Rafko, and his wife, Carmela. Mikey was dressed in a baggy blue tee that hung loose over his khaki shorts, and Carmela had on the usual triple-click bra from Victoria's Secret under a lime-green top that was about two sizes too small for her. I wasn't sure whether their arrival was a stroke of good fortune or a curse. Certainly, it gave me time to think through my strategy with Elvira.

"Who's this?" Mikey asked when he came up. His eyes never got above Elvira's shoulders.

"Oh, this is Elvira," I replied.

"Elvira. Like in the song?"

I saw Elvira looking at Mikey. He pumped iron every day and it showed, even with his loose-fitting shirt. His blond hair was slicked back and long enough to be worn in a ponytail.

"Like in the song," Elvira replied, putting on her sweet little smile for him. "You like that song?"

"Love it," Mikey replied.

I did a slow burn as he undressed her with his eyes. The next thing I know, Elvira has looped her arm through Mikey's and is leading him across the floor to the juke box and Mikey is pumping quarters in the machine while Elvira is hanging all over him. By this time, my irritation was working over-time. Pretty soon the familiar sounds of "Elvira" came wafting out. Out of the corner of my eye, I could see that Carmela was watching Mikey as closely as I was and had an agitated expression on her face. Both Mikey and Carmela had reputations for flirting a lot, but the common wisdom was they were true to each other. As I watched Mikey and Elvira, I wasn't so sure. The expression on Carmela's face had turned downright ugly and I had visions of her using a sharp object on Mikey when she got him home.

In due course, Mikey and Elvira returned from the juke box. I had no idea how many times they'd punched "Elvira's" number, but unless my counting was off, they were already listening to that song for the fourth time. I slid off my stool and moved over and took Elvira's hand and squeezed. She squeezed back, which was a good sign.

"Don't you just love this song?" Elvira gushed. She put one arm around Mikey and the other around me. She had a smile on her face and seemed to be having a good time, but somehow, her eyes weren't smiling even now. She had that strange look again. Maybe it was her tragic life; I thought.

Carmela maneuvered her way around and wedged herself between Mikey and Elvira. She kept time with the music, but her eyes were like two coals. Serves you right, Mikey, you bastard. I thought again about the trouble he'd be in when they got home and did a clap in my mind.

"This is the first time I've seen you in here, David," Mikey said.

Oh, thanks a lot, Mikey. After everything I'd told Elvira. With my well-developed peripheral vision, I saw Elvira staring at me with those eyes that both turned me on and spooked me out just a little.

"I've been in here lots of times," I protested. "I guess we've just been on different schedules."

"That must be it," Mikey said, winking at Elvira and slapping me on the shoulder. Before taking his hand away, he squeezed my shoulder muscles a couple of times. "Say, partner," he said, "you need to start working out. You're a little soft, there."

God damn it, Mikey, keep your stinking observations to yourself. Just because I have interests beyond going to the gym every day.... "I work out," I said defensively.

"Yeah? Where do you go?"

"That new place south of town."

Mikey grinned knowingly. "I thought you just played golf. How many rounds do you play in the average week?" He poked me in the chest this time.

"I don't know. Maybe two."

"Aw, you play more than two!" Mikey said emphatically. "You must play four or five. You ought to rotate, golf one day, workout the next. Tiger, Phil, those guys, they work out every day and it shows with their games. They're the main reason the PGA has this big workout trailer at every tournament stop these days."

I just grunted. I should be used to Mikey by now. Always running his mouth in front of people he'd never met and screwing things up for others. I remembered how it was with my other dates. It was like he took it on himself to run a professional critique of every woman he saw me with. Her dress, her body. And if I took her back to my place, he always seemed to know how long she stayed. I felt constantly under the microscope. Now Carmela, she was a little different. She was into her body, sure, but there seemed to be more to her, more substance. I had the feeling she liked me, too. Maybe that's what drove Mikey nuts. Jealousy. I decided to try to change the subject before he loused things up any more with Elvira.

"End of an era," I said nostalgically. "No more Baker's, no more bikers riding their hawgs through the front door, huh?"

"Yeah, I'll miss this place," Mikey said. "I guess they're keeping this bar, though." He slapped the wood.

I stole a glance at Elvira. The momentary kick of hearing "her song" for five more times seemed to have passed and she was looking more and more jittery. She caught my eye and leaned close. "Can we go?" she whispered again.

I sized things up. Maybe Mikey and Carmela would leave before long and either go home or walk up the street to another place. The last thing I wanted was for them to see me leave with Elvira. If they did, I'd hear about it for the next century. But if I waited them out, and didn't turn the lights on at my place when I got home just in case they decided to wrap it up for the night, then it might work. Elvira looked like she wasn't the type for a lot of preliminaries, anyway.

"In a little while," I whispered back. From the look on her face, I could tell she wasn't a happy camper. Maybe I'd turned her on as much as she'd gotten to me and she wanted to get on with it.

For the next hour, I did my best to keep Elvira entertained. I joked around with Mikey and was careful to include her in the banter. When Mikey moved down the bar to talk with some friends, I was hopeful things were moving in the right direction. Then — it couldn't have been 10 minutes — he was back. To say Elvira was restless now was an understatement. When she excused herself to go to the ladies room, I breathed a sigh of relief. It would buy me a few more minutes of time.

Fifteen minutes passed and Elvira didn't come back, which was alright with me. Women's johns, particularly in crowded bars, always seemed to be busy, and Baker's was filled to the gills with people. Mikey continued to hover nearby, yukking it up with everyone who passed. He showed no signs of getting ready to leave.

"Where's your friend?" Carmela asked.

I gave my patented shrug and said, "Went to the john. Crowded, I guess."

After another 15 minutes, I began to get concerned. Either that line was inordinately long or Elvira had stopped to talk to someone else. The latter possibility concerned me the most, because the place was full of guys ready to hit on any female with a set of knockers.

I told Carmela I was going to the john myself, and if Elvira returned, to tell her where I'd gone. I passed the ladies' room and didn't see her in the line outside the door. I lingered unobtrusively for a few minutes and watched to see who came out. Two ample women, for whom taking a pee was obviously a social occasion, squeezed out the door, followed by a knockout blonde. But no Elvira. I proceeded on to the men's room and was in and out in five minutes. On the way back, I checked the ladies line again, but still no Elvira. I carefully scanned the crowd on the way back to where Mikey and Carmela were, but didn't spot her.

"Did you find Elvira?" Carmela asked when I returned.

"Not really looking," I lied. "I'm sure she's in here somewhere. Probably wedged in a corner talking to an old friend or something."

Elvira had been gone for an hour when I concluded she wasn't coming back. She must have slipped out the back door. I was so depressed at that point that I left the same way and walked home.

Thank you, Mikey! That damned big mouth had really screwed things up for me this time. Insensitive oaf! He could have come over, engaged in polite conversation for a while, and then faded out of the scene when he picked up on what I was doing. But no, he had to hang around and run his mouth and take the edge off the moment. Always thinking of himself, that was Mikey. Murderous thoughts filled my head as I crawled into bed and tried to go to sleep.

■ ■ ■

The next morning, I was working in my garden, still burning over what had happened the night before. I didn't even have her phone number, for crissake! If Mikey had come out his door just then, I would have stuck one of my garden tools into his chest. Or maybe ravaged Carmela before his very eyes! It would have been even sweeter if she'd acted as though she enjoyed it.

I was weeding the petunias when a car pulled up in front of my house. The first thing I noticed was the Sheriff's Department markings on the side. A Deputy in uniform and a plain clothes companion got out and walked up my drive-way. I've always had a fear of authority, and seeing the two of them approach caused my heart to start pounding in my chest like a jackhammer.

"David Bowen?" the uniform asked.

My mouth got dry and I tried to figure out why they could be at my house. I'd had a few beers last night at Baker's, sure, but hadn't been driving. I also went straight home from the bar, and tempted though I was, hadn't trashed Mikey's place or done anything like that.

"Yes," I said, running my tongue over my lips and straight-ening up to my full five-ten height, "I'm David Bowen." I hoped that my voice wasn't quavering.

"I'm Deputy Conway and this is Detective Tessler. We'd like to talk to you for a few minutes if we may."

I looked at one of them, then the other. The plainclothes guy really made me nervous. I knew that the county had exactly one Detective, and here he was, standing in my garden. My nerves were already frayed, and it didn't help any that he was eyeing me suspiciously and looking like he was about to slap the cuffs on me. This can't be happening, I thought. First Mikey screws up my chances of scoring with Elvira and now this.

"There was an incident in town last night," the uniform said. "We think you have some knowledge of the person we believe might have been involved."

I put my hand against a tree to steady myself. What is he talking about? "I was in Baker's Bar all last night," I protested. "You must have the wrong man."

He studied me without smiling. "No, we want to talk to David Bowen. That's you, right?"

"Yes," I said tentatively.

"You talk to anyone while you were in Baker's?"

My mouth felt like flannel now. I forced the words out. "I talked to a woman named Elvira for a while. And my neighbor, Mikey Rafko, and his wife." I waved a hand in the direction of his house. "They were there, too."

"What did this woman — you called her Elvira? — look like?"

I thought about it for a moment. Having the law standing in my garden interfered with my normal thought processes. I gathered my wits about me and said, "She was maybe five-six or five-seven, long black hair, good figure." Just describing her got me aroused again.

The uniform and plainclothes guy looked at each other, then the uniform said, "And she told you her name was Elvira?"

"Yeah, like in the song."

The two lawmen exchanged glances yet again and then the Detective asked, "Did she come on to you?"

I looked at him. It sounded so cheap when he put it like that. "I don't know if I'd put it that way," I said, a little defensively. "There was a mutual attraction, if that's what you mean."

"So she seemed interested in you?"

"Yes, she did," I said, defiantly this time. He acts like that's unusual, I thought. Mikey's comments flashed through my mind and I started to get mad all over again.

Jesus, I wish that Detective would stop staring at me, I thought nervously. I was fidgeting when he asked his follow-up question. "What did you talk about?"

"Things," I replied. "Small talk, mostly. Things people talk about when they're getting to know each other."

"Give me an example."

"Well, at first she thought I might be a psychic because I called her Elvira."

He smiled. "You called her that first?"

"Yeah," I said defensively, "because she kept playing that old song. Plus she kind of looked the way I envisioned Elvira looking. I guess it was subliminal or something. When she admitted her name really was Elvira, I was blown away."

The Detective continued to smile and was scribbling in his small notebook. "You talk about anything else?" he asked without looking up.

I'm not sure whether he bothered me more when he was staring or grinning like I was some damn fool. I thought about his question for a minute. "My ex-wife," I said. "We talked about my ex and why we broke up." I didn't want to get into details here. The conversation with Elvira was all puffing at this point, the way guys do to impress women. Like boasting that they have a big boat even though they didn't have one. That sort of thing. "Oh," I continued, "we talked about her former husband, too, and how he died."

The Detective looked up at me with new interest. "That must have been interesting. What did she say?"

My mind was racing. I didn't want to get into the details of our conversation, but saw no way around it. "She thought a guy she met — she said he was a psychic — might have had something to do with his death."

Both law officers had smirks on their faces again. "A psychic?" said the uniform.

"Yeah, you know, one of those people who can foresee the future?"

"Did she say anything about her husband being found dead in the woods with knife wounds to his side?"

I felt my eyes widen and instinctively put a hand down and felt my ribs. For a moment I couldn't speak. "No," I finally said in a voice I was sure was unsteady. "She said she thought the psychic might have slipped him something."

The Detective looked at his uniformed companion, pursed his lips, and shook his head. "The only thing the poor bastard was slipped was an eight-inch stiletto between his ribs."

Out of the corner of my eye, I saw Mikey come out of his house and look at us quizzically. He probably saw me talking to the officers and was curious about what was going on. I was anxious for some reinforcements at that point given the direction our conversation was taking.

"That the neighbor you mentioned?" the uniform asked, following my eyes.

"Yeah. Hey, Mikey! Come over here and meet these gentlemen. They're asking some questions about who we talked to in Baker's last night."

Mikey came over and stuck out a hand. "Mikey Rafko," he said in his usual confident manner. The two lawmen introduced themselves.

"Mikey, I was just telling these gentlemen that we were together last night at Baker's."

Mikey looked at me and then proceeded to correct what I'd just said. "Not really together. We didn't come or leave as a group. My wife, Carmela, and I bumped into David at the bar. He was making a play for some slutty-looking woman." He looked at me with a leer on his face and slapped me in the shoulder with the back of his hand. He must have noticed the hurt look on my face because he added, "Sorry, partner, but you can do better."

Mikey was at it again. Trying to make Elvira out to be a whore or something. That was a real joke coming from a guy who was married to a woman like Carmela. I did a slow burn, but held my tongue.

"But you did talk."

"Sure, I always talk to my neighbor."

"How late did you stay in Baker's?" the Detective asked.

Mikey answered for us both. "Carmela and I left about 12:30," he said. He looked at me. "What time was it when Elvira ditched you? About 11:00? And then you snuck out a half-hour or so later."

"I didn't *sneak* out," I protested.

"I meant when you left," Mikey said. He probably didn't think I noticed, but I was sure he winked at the Detective.

The uniform and the plainclothesman seemed not to pay attention to Mikey's comments, but asked me, "Where did you go after you left Baker's?"

"I walked home."

There was a lull in the conversation, and I was still sulking over Mikey's insulting comments when the Detective addressed me again. "You said this woman had black hair, is that right?"

"Yeah, that's right. Black as coal. Why do you care about her hair?"

"We believe the woman you were talking to was Melissa Crier. She escaped from an institution for the criminally insane down in Indiana. She had fire-engine red hair the last she was seen."

Holy shit, I thought, grabbing my ribs again, she seemed so normal. Well, maybe not completely normal, but not the kind of woman who'd be committed to an institution. Maybe he was lucky she didn't come back from the john in Baker's.

"What was she in the institution for?" Mikey asked, showing his penchant for getting to the bottom of things.

"I guess you didn't hear our earlier conversation. She was convicted of killing her husband."

Mikey looked at me speechlessly for the first time since I've known him, then recovered and said in a take-charge voice, "My friend here has told you all he knows about that woman. I told you she struck me as something of a whore. We don't know anything else. We only met her in Baker's. I told you she ditched my friend here."

The Detective looked at Mikey, then at me, and then back at Mikey. "We're trying to establish a timeline. We believe Melissa Crier, or Elvira if you prefer, stopped at another bar up the street after leaving Baker's last night. As best we can tell, she picked up a guy there and left with him. His body was found this morning. He died from knife wounds to the side."

THE ROCKS

Hal Craven stared at the wet rocks that lined the steep river bank, oblivious to the beads of water that collected on his cap and trickled down the back of his neck. Occasionally he would sneak a glance in Mac's direction. When he did, a jumble of emotions flooded his consciousness. Guilt was not among them, though. The betrayal had been too great, too personal, to allow for guilt.

Mac stood under the open hatchback of the Ford Explorer, out of the weather, fussing with his equipment. He examined some caddis flies, checked his double-taper line, organized a tan canvas vest with flapped and zippered pockets that held the small tools of a fly fisherman's trade.

Drizzle continued to ooze from a sky that was the color of old pewter. It hung so low an artful backcast would tickle its soft underbelly. Hal inhaled the aroma of the dripping jack pines that surrounded the small clearing where they were parked, and found it difficult to tear his eyes from the slick, glistening rocks. The Ice Age's gift to him.

"Maybe we should wait for a while," Mac called. "See if this crap blows through."

Hal heard the words, but they sounded far away, like some unpleasant noise he was subconsciously determined to filter out. He didn't want to wait. Not when everything was going according to plan. Better even. They were alone at the place where they always accessed the river on their fishing trips, and he'd gotten lucky with the wet conditions. It was almost too perfect.

"Well, what do you think?" Mac asked.

Hal hated the thought of delay. Finally he looked away from the rocks and toward Mac. "You're probably right," he said.

"How many opening days does this make for us?" Mac asked after they'd settled into the front seat of the Explorer. "Fifteen?"

Hal wasn't in the mood for small talk, but tried to act normal, casual even. "I was thinking about it earlier," he forced himself to say. "I believe it's 17."

"Seventeen years." Mac gazed through the windshield at the soggy landscape and shook his head. "We've had some times, haven't we?"

"Yeah, a lot of memories," Hal said, looking out the window on his side so Mac wouldn't see the expression on his face. The phony sentimentality made him want to puke.

Mac wiped some dust from the dash and fiddled with the radio dial, stopping at an oldies station. After a few minutes he said, "You know, sometimes I regret leaving the firm."

Hal rolled his eyes and grunted. "It's the first time I've heard you say that. Why the second thoughts now, three years later?"

"I don't know," Mac said. "It was our baby and all, and the people are still like family to me." He paused for a minute and then continued. "Remember back in our fraternity days when we decided to go to law school and then set up our own shop after getting some training at one of the big firms?"

Yeah, Hal remembered all right. Cameron MacNeill with his privileged background and family contacts had gotten into a national law school while Hal wound up working his way through a no-name place that was firmly buried in a lower tier. Guess who had the pizzazz at cocktail parties? Now the hypocrite was talking about partnership and family. What would come next? Another lecture about Hal's drinking? More hollow promises of legal business from his company? The damn jerk had no conscience, which was going to make this a lot easier for him. Maybe they'd shared some good days in the past, but things had changed, and the changing had been Mac's doing, not his.

Hal squeezed out a snicker. "Hey, you took the money and ran," he said.

"That's not fair," Mac shot back, looking hurt.

Hal shrugged. "You're not going to tell me you haven't done well at L-Tech, are you?"

"No," Mac said, "I'm not saying that at all. I've done very well, but that's not the reason I left. I just needed a change."

Hal's mind flashed back to when Mac had announced he was leaving the law firm, just as things had begun to slide downhill. "Whatever," Hal said. "It's history now."

After a couple of minutes of silence, Mac asked, "Is the firm going to make it?"

Hal's head snapped toward Mac. "What are you getting at?" he asked. "You want me to say things would be different if Cameron MacNeill were still at the firm? That Cameron MacNeill had been the main guy all along. That what you want me to say? Well maybe what our firm has been going through lately has nothing to do with your leaving. Losing a growing client to a big law firm happens these days. And as I recall, you're the one who hired that dogcrap young associate who got us sued."

"Jesus, Hal, you're taking my question the wrong way. I'm just concerned, that's all. Is something wrong? You seem edgy."

"No," Hal said, trying to rein in his churning resentments. "It's just this damned weather."

Mac removed his slouch hat and pulled a leather-covered journal from the center console. He shifted his position so he was leaning against the driver-side door and began to write. Hal glanced over, but the pages were shielded from his view. A Johnny Cash classic drifted from the radio. The one about going to Jackson to mess around.

Mac looked up. "You know, when the Man in Black passed on, that was really the day the music died."

Hal nodded. "Yeah, he was the best." What he really wanted to do, though, was give the radio a hard kick. Those lyrics were the last thing he wanted to hear. But maybe it was good to be reminded about the messing around. Helped him maintain his edge.

Hal snuck another glance at Mac. He didn't see him regularly these days, but the guy seemed to be aging awfully fast. His hair was thin and his skin didn't have the same healthy glow. He was rich as hell, though. Women liked that. If a man had money, the other stuff didn't seem to matter much.

Mac finished writing and slipped the journal back into the console. "How much longer should we give it?" he asked.

Hal turned to him, his brow furled. "You're not thinking about bailing out, are you?"

"No, it's just that...."

"You got a hot date tonight?" Hal asked. "You divorced guys, always on the hunt." He fought to keep the edge out of his voice as he thought about Mac and his wife, Karen. "You've found someone, right?"

"Hey, if I had, you'd be the first to know."

"Would I?" Hal asked.

"What's that supposed to mean?"

Hal forced a grin. "Who's being touchy now? All I meant was that sometimes things change, people change."

"We've known each other too long to change. Shared too much."

Hal's fingernails dug into his palms. That was the problem, the sharing. It had become so obvious lately. The lingering hugs whenever Mac and Karen saw each other, the tender glances. Then there was the long lunch they'd had at Rizzo's the day he'd had Karen followed two months ago. He had pictures of them sitting at a back table, for crissakes, looking at each other like a couple of moonstruck teenagers, her hand on his. How many other lunches had there been? How many hotel rooms?

Mac lowered the window on his side and stuck out a hand. "You know, I think it's stopping."

Hal stepped out of the Explorer. Mac was right. His pulse quickened again at the sight of the rocks. Things were back on track.

"We'll kill ourselves if we try to get down to the river from here today," Mac said, staring at the river bank. "Maybe we should go upstream where it's not as steep."

Hal knew he couldn't let this opportunity slip away. "And fish elbow-to-elbow with all those other guys?" he said. "C'mon. We've always gone down this way."

"But not in these conditions."

Hal played his hole card. "Look, if you want to be a wuss about it, go ahead. I'm fishing here." He looked at Mac and snickered. "Just don't forget to pick me up later, Millie."

Mac gave him a long look. "Okay. You're nuts, but I'll stay and bail you out as usual."

"Yeah, right."

Hal hefted his new Orvis split bamboo fly rod and admired the feel. The rod he couldn't afford, but had bought with the new credit card he'd managed to get a few weeks ago. He was tired of sacrifice. Besides, when he turned his law practice around, a grand for a fly rod would be chickenscratch. He slipped the rod back into its case and slung it over his shoulder. Might as well protect it, he thought; he wouldn't be using it today anyway.

"Okay, Rambo, lead off," Mac said.

Hal looked at him. "That's a change. What happened to Mac the troop leader? The take charge guy?"

Mac just shrugged and waved his hand for Hal to proceed. Hal had counted on Mac taking the lead as usual, but now he'd have to adjust. He forced a chuckle and started down the bank, moving gingerly, and immediately lost his footing. "Whoa!" he cried, trying to sound as though he were having the time of his life.

Slowly they picked their way down the treacherous slope, slipping on a rock here, stopping to regain their balance there. Hal led the way, keeping an eye peeled for the right place. He knew he had to make it happen now. It would be dry later, and his advantage would be gone. The slick rocks were his friends.

Hal selected a route that would take them over a large crowned boulder that looked as smooth as glass. And slippery from the rain. When he reached the boulder, he stepped up and faked a slip as he started across.

"Damn!" he muttered as one knee cracked against the rock.

Mac came up behind him and placed a hand on his shoulder. "You okay?"

Hal squatted and rubbed his knee for a moment. "Yeah, just a little bump."

"Well, be careful," Mac said.

Do it now, Hal told himself. As he rose, he deliberately let his feet slide off the rock and lurched wildly backward, arms flailing. When his hand touched Mac's leg, he grabbed and yanked hard as though reflexively trying to break his fall. Everything turned to slow motion. Hal's back hit the rock, causing pain to shoot through his body, and he saw one of Mac's legs fly into the air. Then he heard a heavy thud as flesh and bone slammed against the rocks. A thud that would be sickening to most, but rang in Hal's ears like the lyrics from a favorite song.

Hal looked back at the twisted body lying among the rocks. "Mac, you okay?" he asked. "Mac?"

Cameron MacNeill's glassy eyes stared at the sky and Hal saw a thin trickle of blood oozing from his head. The jagged point of a nearby rock loomed like the weapon of an avenging angel. He'd done it! Don't panic now, he told himself, everything had to look natural. Was the head injury fatal? Hal didn't dare hit him again; the medical examiner surely would notice that. He had to trust that the rocks had done their job. Think. Should he call for help? Yes, that's what he needed to do. He punched at the numbers on his cell phone, misdialing on the first attempt.

Now show concern, Hal told himself. Get something to cover the body. He scrambled up the steep bank, slipping and banging his knees on the rocks. His heart pounded and sweat soaked his clothes. He found an old blanket in the back of the Explorer, and begun to pick his way down the rocky incline again when he remembered the journal. Could Mac have become suspicious and written something about him? Hal raced back to the vehicle and wrenched open the front door. He snatched the journal from the console and fumbled through the pages, hands trembling. Karen's name appeared in one entry, and a recent one, too. The sonofabitch! Sweat stung Hal's eyes as he began to read:

Saturday will be my last opening day. The doctors leveled with me. The cancer is too far advanced. I told Karen two months ago after she'd noticed my hair. She's been wonderfully supportive. Maybe I should have asked Hal to join us at Rizzo's that day when we met to talk about my condition, but we decided not to tell him until after Saturday. It wouldn't help. So much has gone wrong for him lately, and there was just no use spoiling his opening day. Karen's so devoted to him. They're so lucky to have each other and....

THE NOVELTY OF DECEIT

Malcolm Chance loosened his bow tie and waited for the computer to power up. Man, what a day. The exhilaration over closing on the sale of his company, followed by the black tie gourmet society dinner that evening at which speakers fought over the podium to extol his virtues as Man of the Year. Through it all, the sommelier kept his glass filled with some of the greatest vintage port ever produced. He grinned and shook his head. Being on top certainly had its burdens.

His inbox showed 47 new emails. There were the expected congratulatory messages from friends and business colleagues, and a few from jokers who suddenly acted like they were his friends. Newsmax bulletins and health alerts seemed to appear every six entries. Some of that stuff was good, but goddamn, the volume! He came to a long email from his financial advisor, Marshall Paige. As he read it, he could just see old Marshall hunched over his computer, shitting his pants at the prospect of the fees he'd earn by having all that money to invest.

He continued to scroll down, and when he came to some spam, he barely paused. An ad for an online university. Trash bin. A weekly update from an investment service. Trash bin. A promotion for Cialis. *Cialis, for crissake!* He hadn't needed that stuff for months, not since he cut a deal to sell his company for $352 million. If that didn't get the blood pumping in your dick, nothing would.

Malcolm chuckled at the thought and sat with his finger poised over the mouse, ready to send the next bit of spam to its fate in cyberspace. He almost blipped off an email, but held up when something about it caught his eye. He studied the words on the subject line. "I know what you did," it read. What the hell was this? The sender's name, if he could call it that, was identified as "tdta." It looked like one of those indecipherable abbreviations kids use when texting each other. He manipulated his mouse, looking for the rest of the message or an attachment. That's all there was. Just those five words.

He leaned back in his chair and stared at the screen for a long time. Maybe it was from his friend, Cam Sutherland, who knew he'd banged that blonde at the bachelor's party two weeks ago and was trying to dump cold water on his big day. If it was, he didn't have to worry because he had enough on the prick to keep him quiet. It was like that old Cold War doctrine, MAD. Mutually Assured Destruction. If Cam told anyone about Malcolm's indiscretions, he knew he'd face overwhelming retaliation.

Malcolm continued to study the email, then walked across the room to a window and looked down at Lake Shore Drive 10 floors below. Normally, it was one of his favorite scenes, with bumper-to-bumper traffic creating bands of light as cars snaked through the "S" curve along one of the world's great skylines. He rested a hand on the high-powered telescope and stared out, deep in thought. Nothing registered with him — not the lights, not the movement of the cars, not the pounding surf on the other side of the Drive.

Finally he roused himself and craned his neck so he could see the building with the unit he had a bid on. It was a spectacular co-op with the same great view but a lot more space. With just two of them, they didn't need 9,000 square feet, but hell, what good was money if you couldn't flaunt it?

He went to the bar and held a decanter of port up to the light. He tasted it; not quite the same as what they served at dinner, but still pretty damn good. He poured a glass and settled into his favorite green leather chair. As he sipped the port, his eyes flicked from the phone to his computer and back to the phone. He thought of Celia and suddenly he needed to hear her voice. His friends referred to her as his trophy wife. Whatever. All he knew was that he loved it when heads jerked around like a bunch of bobble-head dolls every time she walked into a room. To be honest, it made him a little jealous, too. But when word got around that he'd sold his company for mega bucks, women started looking at him like he was some goddamned Hollywood stud. Now he was as much the center of attention as his wife.

He picked up the handset and dialed Celia's number. After the usual small talk, they lapsed into phone sex. By the time he got off the call, he was ready to jump on a flight to Florida and nail her right there on the beach. Wouldn't that be great? A gentle breeze off the Gulf, the moon shimmering on the water, the excitement created by the possibility of some hapless soul out for a midnight stroll stumbling upon them when they were bare-assed naked. He laughed at the thought and it made him horny as hell.

His libido slowly receded and he stared at his computer some more. He walked over and brought up the email again. "I know what you did."

■ ■ ■

"See?" said Pac Lorenzo as his long, bony finger pointed at the bottom of the window on his monitor. "At the end of every message, there's always a way to unsubscribe." He looked up with a sly grin. "Unless you bookmarked a porno site, that is."

Malcolm ignored Pac's smart-ass comment. He knew how to unsubscribe emails, too; he just didn't have the patience for it. Plus having his old IT chief over to do the grunt work gave him a perfect opportunity to pick his brain without appearing too obvious.

He watched Pac work his way through site after site, unsubscribing him whenever he gave the signal. He'd always wondered why the buyer of his business didn't want the guy. Too quirky, he supposed. He weighed all of 120 pounds soaking wet and his bald head looked perennially buffed. His name — if he had a formal first name, Malcolm couldn't recall it — came from his affinity for the video game, Pac-Man. Hundreds, maybe thousands, of video games had come and gone since Pac-Man was introduced 30 years earlier, but it remained his favorite. No one ever claimed to have beaten Pac at the classic video game.

"Pac," Malcolm said casually, "every email leaves a trail, right?"

"Absolutely," he replied, continuing his work at the keyboard. "Why do you ask, Boss?"

"Just wondering." A little while later, Malcolm probed again. "I heard that a sender who knows what he's doing can conceal his identity if he wants to."

Pac snorted. "It's easy to use a hokey name on an email. But I bet I could still trace him." Two more commercial solicitations bit the dust. "You thinking of sending some hot babe a late electronic valentine and want to cover your tracks, Boss?" Pac's grin had morphed into a leer.

Malcolm laughed and gave him the "unsubscribe" signal again.

"Or is it the other way around?" Pac asked, animated by the lewd possibilities. "Some women like to send rich dudes love notes suggesting all kinds of kinky things. You been getting love notes, Boss?"

Malcolm laughed again and thought about the five-word email with the sender's funny name. "No," he said, "I guess I'm missing out on the fun. But I have a friend who's been receiving screwy messages every now and again. I was just wondering."

"You want me to help him find out who the sender is?"

Malcolm shrugged. "I'll ask him. How would you go about tracing something like that?"

Pac flashed a toothy grin. "Easy," he said, "it's all in the headers. Here, I'll show you." His fingers flew into motion again and moments later the screen filled with what looked like a bunch of gibberish. "See," Pac said, pointing to a line, "there's the sender. And that's his ISP."

"What's an ISP?"

"Internet service provider. You know, AOL, Comcast."

Malcolm studied the screen. "You picked an easy one, Pac. You already know who that sender is. How about if a person were trying to conceal his identity?"

Pac held his shirt collar over part of his face and looked at Malcolm with a sinister expression. "Like if he were black-mailing you or something?" He erupted in a high-pitched cackle that convulsed his whippet-like body.

Malcolm couldn't help but smile. "Yeah," he said. "Hypothetically, something like that."

When Pac regained control, he said, "I bet I could identify the sender even then. It might be harder if he sent the message from a public library or something. You want me to help your friend, Boss?"

Malcolm shrugged again. "I'll ask him." He had enough knowledge of computers to know that an email could be resuscitated from the trash bin even though it had been deleted. He was tempted to come clean with Pac and have him try to trace the message, but then thought better of it. If it wasn't a prank, he wouldn't want a busybody like Pac to know about it.

■ ■ ■

Malcolm let out a weary sigh as the cab pulled up in front of his building. He'd spent the entire day at Marshall Paige's office interviewing money managers. Marshall's idea was to split the money up, with four managers following different investment philosophies, each having responsibility for $60 million of the after-tax proceeds. Marshall would supervise them and have direct responsibility for the rest.

What a bunch of sharks, Malcolm thought. That hedge fund guy wanted a 3% management fee plus 20% of the profits. That was a hell of a lot of money. He noticed there wasn't any symmetry to the deal, either. The guy just sat there like a bloated carp when Malcolm suggested he shoulder 20% of any losses, too.

The temporary doorman held the door for him and handed him a stack of mail. Sharp young man, Malcolm thought. Elliott something or other and a pretty good stand-in for old Preston who was recuperating from a heart attack. Security was important to him and the other residents and it looked like this guy didn't miss much. He wondered if the new building — assuming he got the unit — had people who were as good.

Malcolm stepped off the elevator and walked down the hall to his study. As he put his briefcase down, he noticed a stain on the eighteenth century end table. He muttered under his breath and got a cloth and wiped it off. People were so damned careless, setting a glass on centuries-old wood without using a coaster.

It was after six. Another few days of getting his financial affairs in order and he could head to Naples to join Celia. Their second anniversary was right around the corner and he had to get her something special. Maybe a diamond pendant or something from Tiffany. He could get a rock someplace else for less money, but there was something about that blue box.

He eyed the port in his decanter. He loved the stuff, but did have one rule: he drank port only after eating and he hadn't had anything since Marshall served them those crappy dried-out sandwiches. He put ice cubes in a glass and filled it with the single malt scotch that his friend in London had sent as a gift. After adding a splash of water, he moved to his computer and turned the power on. It had been a week since that email and the feeling he got in the pit of his stomach every time he logged in had gradually subsided.

There were 22 new emails. Pac's "unsubscribe" blitz had cut down on the volume of spam, but obviously hadn't eliminated it. He scrolled down, unsubscribing to more unwanted communications and taking the time to read emails from friends. One from his old sales manager passed on the latest joke. A leading software firm had come out with a new breast implant — called the iBoob — that could both store and play music and was priced according to cup size. It was considered a major social breakthrough, the punch line went, because women always complained that men stared at their breasts and never listened to them. Malcolm howled with laughter. He'd have to pass that one on to his golfing buddies.

He blipped off five more pieces of spam. Then his finger froze over the mouse as another email from "tdta" appeared at the bottom of the window. He could see "Mickey, I have proof" on the subject line. He stared at it for a few seconds, then hastily scrolled down so he could read the full message. The additional words "I'll be in touch" appeared.

Malcolm could feel his temples pounding. He leaned back in his chair and closed his eyes. He sat there for a long time, and when he finally opened them, he screamed, "You sono-fabitch! Who the fuck are you?" He wanted to strangle the cocksucker! He looked at his hands; they were shaking. Calm down, he told himself, get control of yourself. He rose and gave his chair a violent shove, then walked over to the bar and poured another scotch. He took a big swallow and refilled his glass.

Mickey. The email referred to him as Mickey. He hadn't gone by that nickname for over 25 years. His father had hung the moniker on him when he was four, saying Malcolm didn't fit a hell-raising boy from Chicago's west side. As he got older, the name grew on him, too. It played to the image he was trying to cultivate of the gunslinger quarterback of the high school football team. Combined with his last name, Chance, it conjured up all sorts of images. His favorite was, "Take a chance, Mickey."

He put all that behind him when he enrolled in law school and distanced himself from his father's life. Now someone was raising his past. It was like the creep was stalking him, watching him. Did he know about the patent, too? That had been the first thing to enter his mind when he saw the first email. But who could know? He'd been so careful, confiding in no one, leaving no tracks. And why now, after all these years?

He looked at the bottle of scotch, but didn't refill his glass. He needed a clear head. He pulled out a legal pad and began to make a list of names.

■ ■ ■

Malcolm sat at a table at Gibsons and waited for Henry Crocker to show. When he called and proposed lunch, his former law partner seemed stunned to hear from him. Crocker tried to put him off, pleading workload. That added to Malcolm's suspicions and he persisted, saying he'd buy to celebrate his closing. He gave Crocker a choice of dates and finally he relented.

Malcolm glanced at his watch; Crocker was late. As Malcolm sipped his wine, he recalled his father sitting around the kitchen table with his wannabe friends. One of them would inevitably say he could always tell if a man were lying by watching his eyes. The others would nod in agreement, as if the pronouncement came right from stone tablets. Malcolm had forgotten most of the drivel they spouted, but always remembered about the eyes. He wanted to look into Henry's baby-blues.

Crocker rushed in, 20 minutes late, and dropped into a chair opposite Malcolm. "Sorry," he said. "Couldn't get out of that damn meeting."

Malcolm smiled. "I thought you'd have more time these days without department head responsibilities."

Crocker rolled his eyes. "Busier than ever. You'd never know we were in a recession."

"Well," Malcolm said, studying him, "as I've always said, talent attracts clients. I haven't seen you for a while. You're looking good." Malcolm really thought Crocker looked like shit. He was tense and fidgety and his shirt looked like it had been worn for three days. His weight seemed to be up, too.

"Thanks," Crocker mumbled as he looked around the room. "Not getting enough exercise, though."

"Join me for a drink?"

Crocker looked at Malcolm's wine glass and then gave the waiter elaborate instructions for a dirty martini. Malcolm listened and decided Crocker hadn't changed one damn bit. He'd been removed as head of the firm's patent law practice two years earlier because of his drinking and was still hitting the hard stuff.

"Sam take good care of you?" Crocker asked. Sam was Sam Kopecki, the firm's lead estate planning lawyer. Malcolm had met with him before catching a cab to Gibsons.

Malcolm watched Crocker's hands nervously crease and recrease his placemat. He forced a laugh and said, "He told me my estate wouldn't have to pay a dime of taxes if I died in 2010. Put it off until a later year and my heirs could kiss 55 percent of the estate goodbye."

"And your decision was?" Crocker took a sip of his martini and began to study his menu.

"I told him I was going to hang around a while and depend on him to save me."

"You've got a lot to save, I hear." Crocker continued to look at his menu. "What did you sell for again?"

"More than a peppercorn as my old law school professor used to say." Malcolm perused his own menu and held it so he could study Crocker. He recalled that quaint saying his English friend always used when he was envious: "It certainly makes my eyes green." Crocker's eyes were the color of jade.

They got their orders in and Crocker asked the waiter to bring him another martini. "Business is where the money is," he said. "I've always wondered how my life might be different if some guy had invited me to join his company like Phil Byers did with you."

Malcolm nodded politely, but inwardly seethed. The difference, Malcolm wanted to say, was that he saw an opportunity and seized it, unlike a fucking technician like you, Henry. And Byers didn't *invite* him to join his company; he *proposed* it after Byers told him about his invention and Malcolm got a sense of the potential and what it would mean for the future of the business. He didn't go by Mickey any more, but the old instincts were still there.

Crocker took a long sip of his fresh drink and a few seconds later took another sip. As Malcolm watched him, he thought about how he'd cozied up to the guy around the time he was preparing to withdraw from the firm to join Byers. He'd never been close to Crocker, and in fact didn't even like him, but needed someone who could educate him on the intricacies of the patent laws. Crocker was more than happy to talk about the field with his new friend. He spoke in hushed tones about "prior art" and "novelty" and "non-obviousness" like they were ecclesiastical terms straight from the Bible.

The waiter brought their food and Crocker attacked his chicken Caesar like he hadn't eaten in a week. Between bites, he finished his second martini.

"Too bad Byers didn't live to see the fruits of his talent," he said as he waved an arm to get the waiter's attention.

Malcolm tried to look sympathetic. "I guess."

"Did you have any idea he was that unstable when you went into business with him?"

"What do you mean?" Malcolm asked, frowning.

"Sorry, I just meant the way he died. That must have been a shock."

Malcolm shook his head. "No one saw it coming."

"His wife found him, as I recall."

"Son."

"Even worse."

Crocker knew all about the way Byers died. Malcolm had told him after Byers' body was found in his garage hanging at the end of a rope. Why was he raising it again now? The vodka must be working on him. Come on, waiter, hurry up with that third martini.

Crocker stuffed another forkful of lettuce into his mouth. "What do you think pushed him over the edge?"

Malcolm's mouth suddenly felt dry. "I don't know," he said. "I guess he had more problems than anyone realized. His wife had left him and everything."

Crocker nodded as if he knew how that felt. "I assume Byers' death slowed down the patent process. When did you file again?"

What was Crocker doing, trying to trip him up? "You know, Henry," he replied, "I don't even remember. It was so long ago and a lot has happened since then."

Crocker wasn't ready to let it go. "Let's see, it took over three years for the letters patent to issue, as I recall." He counted on his fingers and threw out a month and year.

"That could be right," Malcolm said. "Like I said, I don't remember exactly."

After taking another sip of his fresh martini, Crocker said, "I've been getting even complicated patent applications through in a year-and-a-half to two years."

Malcolm looked at him and forced another grin. "Hey, you're a talent, like I said."

After some conversation about what was happening around the firm, Crocker was back to the patent. "I still don't understand why you didn't hire me." He avoided Malcolm's eyes and concentrated on mopping up the Caesar dressing with a hunk of bread.

"I told you before," Malcolm said, "your billing rate was too high. We were a poor company in those days."

"I would have cut you a deal."

Zeke Bratton was both cheap and 80 years old at the time. His mind had lost its natural inquisitiveness, too, and he could be counted on not to ask too many questions. That fit Malcolm's needs perfectly. The fact Byers knew him helped Malcolm get around his demand that he hire a big name patent lawyer. Zeke went to his grave six years ago and took with him anything he might have suspected.

Malcolm changed the subject. "You still with Brenda?" he asked. Brenda Halperin was Crocker's long-time legal assistant. Four years ago, a private detective photographed them in a hotel room doing all kinds of naughty things to each other. His wife filed for divorce, and after hitting his lawyer with a stack of nine-by-twelve glossies, cleaned him out royally and gained sole custody of their two children.

"Still together," Crocker said in reply to Malcolm's question. "We have a place in the Lincoln Park area."

Maybe that's it, Malcolm thought. Maybe the guy's desperate for cash. But again, how did he find out about the patent? And why did he wait so long to play his hand? "Well, say 'hi' for me," Malcolm said.

Malcolm's wine was warm and his glass was still half full. "You're pretty good with computers, as I recall," he said. "I was talking to a friend the other day. He's been getting wacko emails from a strange address. Do you know how to trace something like that?"

Crocker looked shaken for a second and shrugged. "That's a bit out of my area of expertise."

"I put him in contact with a guy I know in New York. Real wiz who says he can trace just about anything."

Crocker's cell phone rang and he grabbed it like a man who was on edge. He talked for a few seconds and then said, "Malcolm, I'm sorry, I've got to run. My secretary just reminded me I have a two o'clock conference call."

"No problem. Why don't you take off. I'll wait for the bill."

"Thanks," Crocker said, making eye contact for a fleeting second. He gulped down the last of his martini. "Let's do this again soon. My treat next time."

Malcolm watched him cross the room, get his coat, and hurry out. He stared at the door long after Crocker was gone, barely conscious that the waiter had brought the check.

■ ■ ■

Crocker knew. Malcolm wasn't sure how, but it was clear he knew. That was the conclusion he'd reached when he winnowed down his list. His questions about when the application was filed and how long the process took only confirmed his suspicions. Crocker also failed the litmus test from the 'hood. His eyes jumped around in their sockets throughout lunch, like ping pong balls at a lottery drawing.

Did he know about the rejection notice? That was key — the notice that informed Byers his invention did not qualify for patent protection because it lacked novelty. The notice fooled Byers, but if an experienced patent lawyer like Crocker saw it....

He had the Mickey part figured out, too. He'd never told Crocker about his nickname, he was sure of that. In fact, the only time he'd slipped and said anything about his past was when he was out drinking with Byers one night and in a burst of braggadocio, told him about his old days on the West Side. Obviously, that couldn't be a problem anymore. But if Crocker stumbled on to some irregularities in the patent process, he might have checked out Malcolm's background. There were plenty of people in the old neighborhood who would still remember him.

The question was, what to do? Maybe the shot across Crocker's bow when Malcolm told him the story about the guy who could trace emails would scare him off, make him think twice about what he was doing. After all, blackmail, if that's what he had in mind, was a crime.

He glanced at his watch. Shit, he was late for his meeting with Marshall Paige. He glanced down at his ratty jeans and sweater. Screw it, he thought. Other people worried about their dress when they had a meeting with a rich man, not the other way around.

Three days had passed since his lunch with Crocker and all was quiet. Maybe his not-so-subtle tactics had worked. He ran some errands, and after returning to his co-op, checked his phone messages. One was from Adam Lynch, his lawyer, regarding the post-closing adjustments to his deal. Malcolm wasn't too happy when Lynch told him the adjustments in favor of the buyer would come to $690,000. That was a lot of money. After grilling Lynch about why he couldn't cut some sort of deal, maybe offer to split the difference with the buyer, he hung up in a huff.

Malcolm was still fuming when he moved to his computer to check his emails. As soon as he logged in, he was startled to see another email from "tdta." It followed the same pattern as the last one — a teaser in the subject line and the rest of the message below. The subject line read, "You used to get a lot of mail, Mickey." He scrolled down. "How come there were two postcards acknowledging your filing? Wait for my instructions."

He slumped in his chair; that icy feeling in his gut was back. Only a patent lawyer would know that including a post-card with a paper application was standard procedure so the

U.S. Patent Office could acknowledge receipt of the package. Malcolm had gone to great lengths to make the first postcard look authentic. He even flew to Washington, D.C. to mail it so it would have the proper suburban Virginia postmark. When Byers killed himself, he scoured his office to remove evidence. He found a copy of the rejection notice, but not the postcard. Maybe Byers had thrown it out, he concluded.

Malcolm studied the email again. It had come in just after four; it was now four-forty. He exploded from his chair and went to the phone and began to savagely punch in his old law firm's number. The receptionist told him that Crocker wasn't available. When pressed, she said he left about three-fifteen and hadn't returned yet. Yes, she said, he should be back any minute. He declined to leave a message and said he'd call back.

So Crocker was conveniently out of the office at the time the latest email was sent. At some public wifi site, no doubt. Malcolm could feel his jaw muscles tense. He'd been working up to a decision and now knew what he had to do. Crocker probably thought he had Malcolm's nuts in a vice. Well, he'd see whose nuts were in a vice.

He called his travel agent and had her book a first class ticket to Ft. Myers the next morning. He deliberately left his return open. The next call couldn't be made from his home number. It couldn't be made from his cell phone, either. He set the alarm in his co-op and headed down the elevator. The day-shift doorman hailed a cab for him and asked where he was going so he could give the driver instructions. Malcolm almost slipped up and said Union Station, but then caught himself and gave his destination as Fields. He got out in front of the department store — he still couldn't bear to call it Macy's — but instead of going in, walked down the street a block and caught another cab. He felt the quarters in his pocket. He needed to find a pay phone.

■ ■ ■

Malcolm got out of bed and stretched. He'd spent another sleepless night and had been on edge ever since he got to Florida. Celia had noticed it, too. He wondered if Cialis could compensate for tension. Too late now, he thought; his supply was back in his medicine cabinet in Chicago. He closed the French doors quietly so he wouldn't wake his wife and went out on the second floor balcony. The weather was perfect again. The Gulf waters were shimmering under the bright Florida sun and the sand on the wide beach in front of their house gleamed like a coat of fresh white paint.

After a few minutes, he went downstairs to his study. He'd been checking for news every day since he arrived; maybe this would be the day. After scrolling down a dozen entries, he saw an email from his old law firm's managing partner. His pulse jumped. The email was addressed to current and former partners and announced the tragic news. Long-time partner Henry Crocker and one of the firm's legal assistants, Brenda Halperin, had been mugged in Lincoln Park while out running the previous night. Both died of head wounds on the way to the hospital. After the usual platitudes about grief and loss and the fragility of human life, the managing partner concluded by saying that further word about the memorial services and funerals would follow.

Malcolm squeezed his eyes closed. His hands started to shake and suddenly he felt cold in spite of the balmy weather. He pulled the robe tighter and sat back in his chair. Then he looked over at the bar. It was only ten-thirty in the morning, Florida time. He knew Celia would detect alcohol on his breath so he just sat there, staring into space. Suddenly he felt angry. You brought it on yourself, fuckhead! You should have brought your A-game when you decided to mess with him. He wondered how many millions Crocker planned to hit him up for. A lot, probably. He never would have been free of him, either. The guy would have been like a leech, continuing to suck his blood. Who the hell could blame him for putting an end to it?

■ ■ ■

Malcolm sat in a pew with other partners and former partners. The minister seemed to go on forever. And then there were the eulogies. There was no end to them and they extolled the virtues of Crocker like he was some goddamned saint. Not a word about the prick being a drunk and an adulterer and a blackmailer who wanted to strip Malcolm of his wealth and ruin his life. The sanctuary felt hot and he loosened his tie a little when he thought no one was watching. He kept sneaking looks at his watch.

When the service finally ended, Malcolm slipped away as gracefully as he could. He needed to be outside to clear his head, to walk even though the March day was raw with the feel of snow in the air. He turned his collar up and held it around his neck. He was shaking again as he turned south on Michigan Avenue.

The day-shift doorman greeted him as he walked into his building. On the elevator, he remembered how Preston had greeted him like a long-lost friend when he returned from

Florida for Crocker's memorial service. It was comforting to have him back. It was almost like things had returned to normal.

He threw his topcoat on a chair and sprawled out on the sofa. He lay there, looking up at the ornate ceiling. Then he closed his eyes. It wasn't his fault. Crocker was a blackmailer, he told himself again. That was a crime, wasn't it? He was protecting himself, that's all.

It was just like with Phil Byers. He'd been putting the money into the company to keep it afloat, for crissakes, and all Byers did was hit the bottle and disappear for days on end. He just wanted to force him into adjusting the ownership interests to fifty-fifty, as they should have been all along, and then he'd file the application. Maybe he shouldn't have dummied-up that postcard and the rejection notice, but he didn't *kill* the guy. No one could have foreseen that the dumb fuck would go off the deep end. The man was weak, that's all.

He'd treated Byers' family damn well, too. When the business took off like a California brushfire, fueled by the protected market niche the patent provided, he voluntarily paid the family a million dollars in excess of the appraised value of Phil's interest. A lot of people would have just shrugged and said, "tough shit."

Malcolm lay there for a long time with conflicting emotions swirling around in his head. Finally he got up and walked to the bar where he poured a scotch. He sipped the liquor, trying to relax. After a while, he dialed Celia's number, but there was no answer. He tried her cell phone with the same result. Probably on the beach or out to lunch with one of her friends. He looked at his computer; he hadn't checked his email for three days. Maybe he should do that to fill time until Celia got back. He needed to do *something*.

He took the bottle of scotch over to his computer where he went through the usual drill to log in. He refilled his glass, then began to work through the emails. Halfway down the most recent day he saw an email from "tdta" with "Where were you?" in the subject line. He stared at it in disbelief. He scrolled down frantically so he could read the rest of the message. It read, "I'm pissed, Mickey." His heart began to pound as he wildly scanned through the other emails. Near the beginning of the previous day's messages, he found another email from "tdta" with "Meeting" in the subject line and a message below that said, "Mickey, meet me at 8:00 p.m. on the top floor of the IBM Building parking garage. Come alone and don't be late."

He stared at the email for a long time and began to shake again. It was sent after Crocker was killed. "No!" he screamed. "Crocker sent those fucking emails!" He flung his glass across the room and shards flashed in the light when it smashed against the wall. "Crocker did it!" He knocked the computer to the floor and kicked at it. Pieces of the keyboard slithered across the Persian rug. "You sonofabitch!" He kicked the computer again and flailed away at everything in sight. A lamp went flying and furniture broke under his frenzied attack.

Finally he sank down on the leather couch, exhausted. He had trouble breathing. He got up and ran to a window and tried to open it. It didn't budge. Then he remembered. The co-op had all windows permanently sealed to prevent suicides. He flopped on the couch again and began to cry.

■ ■ ■

Malcolm spent two days in bed, not eating, not talking to anyone except Celia when she called. She exploded when he told her that all flights out of O'Hare had been grounded due to a major March blizzard and he wouldn't be coming down until the airport reopened. She reminded him that they were supposed to attend a fancy soiree at the beach club that night and slammed the handset down so hard it made his ears ring. Tears clouded his eyes. He wished he could be with her, to tell her everything, to beg her forgiveness.

After pulling himself together, he spent half the day cleaning up the wreckage in his study. He wondered how he was going to explain to Celia about the broken end table. It had been a gift from her on their first wedding anniversary. Maybe a dealer could replace it. No, he decided; antiques were one of a kind. Repair would be more likely. He gathered up the pieces and frantically looked through some antiques magazines for repair services.

Not knowing what else to do, he called his New York contact — he really did know a private detective there — and asked him to try to trace the emails. When the detective called back, he told Malcolm what he already suspected, which was that the emails most likely had been sent from a wifi site open to the public. A library or something. He said he'd continue to work on it, but wasn't optimistic.

Depressed, Malcolm trudged through the snow to an electronics store on Michigan Avenue where he bought a new laptop to replace his desktop Dell, then returned to his co-op and hooked it up. There were no new emails from "tdta." He knew better than to believe it was over, though. It might never be over. What did the guy want anyway? He'd pay him to go away. Fifty million, more even. But he *had to go away.*

Malcolm was exhausted, but knew he had to do something to take his mind off things, to give himself time to think.

Maybe go to the health club for a workout. Yes, that should help because he hadn't been getting enough exercise lately.

He changed clothes and took the elevator down to the lobby where he asked Preston to hail a cab. With the blizzard, it was the better part of an hour before one arrived. When he finally got to the health club, he worked on the Stairmaster and ran laps around the perimeter and lifted free weights until his upper body shut down. Then he ran some more. He was bone-tired when he finished. Maybe he'd finally be able to sleep when he got home.

After a long shower, he got dressed, put up the hood on his parka, and wrapped his scarf around his neck. Then he ducked out into the driving snow and started what he knew would be a long wait for a taxi. As he stood there, he noticed another man with his back to him who also appeared to be waiting for a taxi. When Malcolm glanced his way again, the man had moved closer and held the drawstring to keep the hood tight around his head. Malcolm said, "If a cab comes along, instead of fighting over it, why don't we double up and split the cost."

The man turned and looked at him, then dropped his hood. Malcolm was surprised to see it was the temporary doorman at his co-op.

"Hey," Malcolm said, "I didn't know you were a member here."

He was so close now Malcolm could almost feel the body warmth. "You don't know who I am, do you?" the man asked.

Malcolm squinted through the blowing snow. "You're Elliott, the guy who stood in for Preston at our co-op. You want to share a cab?"

"I'm Elliott Byers," he said. His eyes looked dead and he pulled a worn leather volume from his pocket with "Philip Byers" embossed on the front. "I've been looking through my father's things and doing some research."

Malcolm blinked a few times, but he was too stunned to say anything.

"The diary tells all, Mickey."

Malcolm started to speak. Then he saw the blade.

M-22

ete Thorsen had been accused of living in the past. His love of oldies when it came to music, his preference for history over other literature. And his affinity for older cars. He drove a 10-year-old green Range Rover, and that was by choice. He just felt that older models had more character. Lapses on the assembly lines and design defects probably had decreased in recent years, but older cars still gave him a feeling of comfort.

So when he entered the parking lot of the Red Apple, the first thing that caught his eye was the beige Corvette parked near the front door with the top down. He pulled into a slot a few cars away, and walked over to examine the vintage convertible. He wasn't an expert on the model years of old 'Vettes, but he'd guess it dated back to the 1960s or maybe the early 1970s. The paint gleamed as though freshly waxed and the leather interior looked exceptionally well-cared for. This certainly wasn't a vehicle in which the owner's dog was a regular passenger and had free rein to leap madly about, yapping at everything and everybody in sight.

He took one last admiring look at the sleek machine, and walked through the door of the ramshackle building. It had been a couple of years since he'd been in the Red Apple, but the place had a familiar look once he was inside. A bar ran the length of the room on the right, and tables for diners filled the rest of the space. A handful of tables was occupied, and people contentedly munched on their cheeseburgers and club sandwiches.

The Red Apple was a fixture on M-22, a landmark where the highway snakes north through Arcadia toward Elberta and Frankfort and places north. Every so often, motorists got a glimpse of Lake Michigan as they wound through stands of timber and the occasional fruit orchard. He'd heard that the old restaurant was slated for renovation, but he liked it the way it was. The dilapidated look somehow fit the place.

The bar itself was vacant except for a couple studying a guidebook intently and an older man at the end. Pete looked at the man without staring. Somehow he looked familiar. Brush cut hair that once was reddish-brown, but now had a lot of gray in it. Blue oxford button-down shirt tucked into his khaki shorts. The man was reading a copy of *The Northern Express,* the free regional newspaper. Pete stole another look at the man, and then began to peruse his menu. He gave the bartender his order — a Miller Lite and a grilled chicken-breast sandwich with a double order of slaw instead of fries.

As the bartender took down his order, Pete asked, "Who owns that Corvette parked out front?"

Without looking up, the bartender jerked his head in the direction of the man with his head buried in the paper. "Gentleman at the end," he mumbled as he headed toward the grill.

The man, apparently having heard the conversation, looked up from his paper. He raised his bottle of Bud in a mock salute to Pete. "You into old cars?" he asked.

"Not as old as yours," Pete replied. He laughed. "My Range Rover is 10 years old, but it's just a pup compared to your car."

The man grunted. "Ten years. It's just getting broken in."

"That's what I keep telling friends who kid me about my bucket of bolts."

The man grabbed his beer and paper and moved down the bar closer to Pete. "You new to these parts?" he asked.

Pete shook his head. "I'm from Chicago, but I've been coming to this area for quite a few years."

"I was in Chicago once. Nice town. Beautiful lake front. The say the mob runs the city, though."

Pete had heard that before and was tired of all the mob stories even though he wasn't a native Chicagoan. He'd practiced law in the city for over 20 years, and had a lot of European clients who visited. They thought Chicago was run by Mafia types, too. Besides visiting Gene & Georgetti's or one of the city's other premier steakhouses, the thing they most wanted to do was to see the old hotel where Al Capone holed up or the garage where the infamous St. Valentine's Day Massacre took place. When he told them that many of the storied places in Chicago history had long since been torn down, they wanted to see the site anyway so they could tell their pals back home that they'd been to the place where it all happened. Old reputations die hard, and Chicago was exhibit number one for that proposition.

"I was in that restaurant along old Route 66, west of the city, when I was there," the man said. "Chicken something.

I forget the whole name." His brows knit together as though he were trying to remember.

"Chicken Basket."

"Huh?"

"Chicken Basket. The name of the restaurant is The Chicken Basket."

"That's it. The Chicken Basket. All kinds of Route 66 memorabilia in there. I like that place." He rubbed his chin. "My name is Elbert by the way — that's with an 'E' — but most folks call me Tod. One 'd.'"

Pete suppressed a grin. If his name were Elbert, he'd go by Tod, too. He accepted Tod's hand, and said, "Pete Thorsen."

"Thorsen," he said. "Thorsen. That Scandihoovian?"

"Norwegian," Pete replied.

"I thought that was a good Scandihoovian name. My mother was part Scandihoovian. Mix of Danish, Swedish and Norwegian. Kind of mongrel Scandihoovian, I like to say."

Pete chuckled. Mongrel Scandihoovian. He'd have to remember that. What did that make him, then? With only Norwegian blood, he must be a purebred.

"Say," Tod asked, "my 'Vette okay when you came in? No weather in the area or anything?"

"Just fine," Pete replied. "Not a rain cloud in sight. I've got to ask you, though, don't you get a little nervous about leaving that car alone with the top down?"

Tod shook his head. "Never had any problem. People know who that car belongs to. They warn me if it looks like rain is moving in. And vandals know better than to touch it." He made the latter comment with the certainty of a man who wasn't to be trifled with.

"How long have you had the car?"

"Let's see," he said, rubbing his chin again. "It'll be 20 years in August."

"Long time," Pete said.

"Those cars were built to last. The Ford Mustang, too. The fellow I bought my machine from said that it was the Corvette used in the old television series, 'Route 66.'"

"No kidding?" said Pete.

"No kidding," Tod replied. He got a crafty look in his eyes. "I verified it, too. It's like President Reagan used to say — 'trust but verify.' There's a metal plate welded underneath the steering column that lists the episodes the car appeared in."

Pete nodded, and held his tongue. Anyone could weld a plate on a car that said anything. Then he said, "I've seen a few reruns of 'Route 66.' I always thought the Corvette in that series was red."

Tod grunted. "A popular misconception! The cinematographers for the series wanted a car that would film well so they insisted on beige. 'Route 66' was shot in black and white, you know. People think the 'Vette was red because that's what the PR guys came up with for their publicity posters. They wanted something with more pizzazz than beige. Red worked on the posters, but not on film. A little trivia for you."

Pete nodded. "Route 66" ran for five or six years back in the 1960s. It featured two guys — the lead was played by an actor named Martin Milner — who followed the venerable old highway looking for adventure. When they came to some town, invariably they discovered a wrong being perpetrated against one or more of the locals, righted the wrong, and then motored on again. It was the modern-day version of the Old West stories where a gunfighter, usually with baggage from the past, would ride into town, save a bunch of homesteaders from a rapacious rancher, and then disappear over the horizon again, leaving behind a love-struck widow or an innocent little boy calling for him to come back. Times change, but not the plot.

Pete thought about the episodes of "Route 66" he'd seen, and said, "I seem to recall that the hero in that series was named Tod, too."

"He was," the man said. "That's how I got my nickname. People started calling me 'Tod' after I bought the Corvette. I kind of like it."

Pete looked at him. "You even look like Martin Milner."

He was obviously pleased with Pete's observation, and said earnestly, "You're not the first one who's made that comment."

"Tod had a sidekick in that show, right?"

Tod nodded. "Guy named Buz. He was played by George Maharis in the early years."

"That's right. Tod and Buz."

"Those guys had a lot of personal integrity. And courage. Nothing rattled the boys in the 'Vette."

They sat quietly for a minute, then Pete asked, "You ever drive old Route 66?"

"That's another misconception," Tod said. "Even though the show was named 'Route 66,' segments took place all over the country." He looked at the bar and wiped a spot with his napkin, "But no, I've never driven old Route 66. That's on my list of things to do before I die, though. One of these days, I'm going to throw some stuff in the 'Vette and just go."

"That would be fun."

Tod got a faraway look in his eyes and said, "You know, that old series was made for television, but the writers based a lot of it on real incidents. Embellished a little, obviously.

But you don't have to drive that old highway to find problems that need solving. Those problems exist right here on M-22."

"That right?" The bartender came with his order. Pete took a bite of his chicken sandwich and looked at Tod when he asked the question.

"You bet it's right. Can't count on the police, either, if you uncover something. Sometimes they don't think there's any real problem, or maybe they lack the resources to investigate. Buz and I ran into plenty of that when we were cruising M-22 together."

"Buz and I?"

Tod's lips tightened and he just sat there. Finally he said, "Yeah, Buz and I. I had a sidekick named Buz for a while."

"The same as in the television show?" Pete asked.

He nodded, still dead serious. "His real name was Karl Stroud, but people started calling him Buz because he rode with me. Was the spitting image of George Maharis, too.

This was getting rich, Pete thought. Two characters named Tod and Buz who cruised M-22 in a Corvette used in the old television series. He wanted to ask how many widows and orphans they'd saved, but seeing the expression on Tod's face, decided to keep his sarcasm in check.

Pete took another bite of his sandwich. While he chewed, he asked, "So you two cruised up and down the highway, just like those guys did on 'Route 66.'"

"Not full time, or anything," Tod replied. "We both had jobs. That left only the weekends."

Pete nodded politely and continued to eat.

"We didn't go looking for trouble," Tod said, "but there's plenty out there, I can tell you that."

Pete finished his sandwich and glanced at his watch. He should get going, he thought. However, he was fascinated by Tod, and anyway, he wanted to hear how his preposterous tale ended so he could regale his old friend, Harry McTigue, at dinner.

"When we found trouble," Tod continued, "we tried to set it right. But as I said a few minutes ago, we brought in the police whenever we could. That didn't always work out. Then we had two choices — just drop the damn thing, or see what we could do ourselves."

Pete waited for Tod to continue.

Elbert — or Tod, if you will — didn't need prodding. With that faraway look in his eye again, he said, "It wasn't the same after we got involved in that case where the mob tried to take over the wine business in northern Michigan."

"What happened?" Pete asked when Tod remained silent for a few minutes.

Tod grimaced and finally said, "It all started when we were talking to a bartender in a joint up on the Leelanau Peninsula one night. He started to tell us this story about a widow who was trying to hold out against efforts by an outfit called GMW Company to buy her grape orchards for a song. Seems her husband died and she was trying to figure out how to pay the estate taxes and still keep the orchards." Tod shook his head and looked at Pete. "You know, if he'd waited until 2010 to die, everything would have been okay," he said in an aside. "That's the year the death tax disappeared, but only for one year. To make matters worse, GMW claimed it had a deal with the husband to sell the orchards to their company for a ridiculously low price."

Pete nodded. The estate tax part rang true. He knew the problems faced by farmers and other small business owners. Adding the mob to the story gave it a new twist.

"Anyway," Tod said, "we started nosing around, trying to find out who was behind GMW and stuff like that to see if we could help the widow. The more we looked, the more suspicious we became. Seems a lot of independent grape growers in the region were having problems similar to the one the widow was facing. A contact in Detroit also told us that some Italian guys — the Gallani brothers — owned GMW. You ever hear of the Gallanis? In those days, mob influence in the Motor City was rampant — numbers, juice, you name it. But small fruit orchards didn't make sense. Buz and I talked about it. We put two and two together and concluded the Gallanis were involved somehow even though we didn't know exactly how."

"Mmm," Pete murmured.

"That made it all the more suspicious," Tod said, "and we alerted the police, but they told us there was nothing illegal about what the brothers were doing. Get a lawyer, they said, it's a civil law thing. Mary Singleton — the widow — wanted to sell when she found out the mob was behind it, but Buz and I talked her out of it. You know, Buz was a former marine and tough as nails. He was in Desert Storm and everything. After talking it over some more, Buz and I decided to go to Detroit to pay the Gallani brothers a little visit."

"That was risky," Pete said. "Those boys in Detroit don't fool around."

"You're telling me. You been in Detroit lately? Get away from the Renaissance Center and the place looks like a damned war zone. We didn't take the 'Vette because we were afraid it would stand out too much. Buz drove his old Caddy, which fit right in. We told an intermediary for the Gallanis that we were coming and said we'd meet them for a sit-down at this little Italian restaurant. I wanted to take weapons, but Buz talked me out of it. He said if they knew we were carrying, we would blow any chance we had of brokering a peaceful settlement. This had to be handled by reason, and if we couldn't get them to lay off Mary that way, there'd be time enough to add muscle later.

"Anyway, about five in the evening, we blow into Detroit in the Caddy and after going to our motel to clean up, we had dinner at another Italian joint. Pasta that was out of this world and sauce to match. We were sitting there feeding our faces when I noticed these four goons at a table over by the wall. They kept giving us the eye even though they pretended they were just looking around. They were done before we were and left. It was as though they'd been watching us and timed their departure for just before we finished. We had a couple of cups of Espresso and settled up for our dinner and walked outside into the parking lot. I can tell you, I was wishing I hadn't let Buz talk me out of carrying heat because I was feeling naked as hell. But the parking lot was empty and I breathed a sigh of relief. We concluded we'd just let our imaginations run away with us at the restaurant.

"When we got back to our motel, we settled in for the night. Buz was flopped on his bed watching Sports Center and I was reading a book. Then I thought I heard something outside. I walked over and opened the curtain just a sliver and saw a car parked in the rear of the lot that wasn't there when we came in. An old police officer once taught me how to size up a situation, and that's what I'd done when we entered the motel lot. Now, though, I'll tell you, I started to get nervous as hell. I didn't know whether it was the guys from the restaurant or what. After a few minutes, I went back to my book, but kept my ears open. Ten minutes later, I took another look-see. The car was gone, but then I spotted it again over near the side of the motel."

The story sounded like a second-rate crime novel, but Pete had to admit it was intriguing. He wondered what episode of "Route 66" it came from as he waited for Tod to continue. The television crime-buster wannabe smoothed his brush cut with the palm of his hand.

"I eased the curtain back and got on my bunk again and pretended to read my book, but my mind was going a mile a minute. Then we heard a loud bang outside our window. Buz and I were off our bunks in a flash. He hadn't been going to the window, but it was obvious he'd been listening for trouble, too. He was on his belly snaking over to the window faster than I could say 'mob.' Neither of us could see anything, so we eased our door open and looked outside. Then we saw it; a concrete block lay in back of the Caddy and there was a big dent in the trunk. Like this," he said as he held his hands up to form a large circle.

"Buz raced out like he was going after a nest of terrorists. I was more cautious, holding back because I didn't know whether those guys were trying to draw us out or what. Finally it looked like the coast was clear, and I joined Buz to look at the Caddy. Buz was seething, I can tell you that. The old marine was coming out in him. He loved that car. I had all I could do to stop him from going after the Gallanis that night."

He took another swallow of his beer and continued. "We thought we'd get some help from the law after what happened to the Caddy," he said, "but the officers who arrived on the scene said it probably was some street punks who vandalized the car. We told the cops we thought it was the Gallanis, but they just laughed at us. I don't know whether they were in cahoots with the brothers or what.

"The next day, Buz was still mad, but had himself under control again. Our sit-down with the Gallanis was supposed to take place at noon. We walk into the restaurant — it looked just like the place where we had dinner the night before, red-and-white checked tablecloths, the smell of garlic in the air — on time but no Gallanis. To make matters worse, no one in the place even admitted to knowing who they were. We realized we were up against a brick wall and finally gave up and drove back home."

Tod ordered another Bud, and sat there alone with his thoughts. "What to do now," he mused. "We kicked it around and decided to survey all of the small grape growers in the area. We found that eight of them had been offered the same deal as Mary Singleton. Three had either accepted the offer or were on the verge of accepting it. We knew we had to act fast. Buz and I called a meeting of all the growers. Every last one showed up, which is an indication of how they viewed our leadership. We talked it through, and in the end, all of them agreed that they weren't going to be pushed around and made a compact not to sell unless everyone sold.

"After the meeting, Buz and I brainstormed about how we could smoke out the Gallanis. We knew the mob had gone legit with a lot of their ventures. Maybe they were trying to corral the wine business in our area. If they were, what they hoped to achieve was still a puzzle. Control over prices, maybe? Or maybe they wanted a legit business through which they could launder their dirty money. We couldn't think of any other motive.

"Then — I don't know, it was maybe a couple of days after our meeting with the growers — Buz was at home alone when he told me he heard this huge blast outside his place. Well, I won't bore you with the details, but someone torched his Caddy. All that was left of that beautiful machine was the charred frame. I'll tell you, even Buz was shook after that happened."

Tod sat there with a pensive expression on his face. "I blame myself for what happened next. It was a couple of days later. The manager of the park where Buz kept his trailer went looking for him because he apparently was delinquent a few days in paying his rent. The guy's a real shit, by the way. A day late and he treats you like some deadbeat." He choked on his words, then regained his composure. "The manager found Buz laying on the floor with a gunshot wound to his head." Tod rubbed a sleeve across his eyes.

"He was shot? What happened?" Pete asked.

Tod collected himself and then said, "Nobody knows for sure. Here's the article that appeared in the *Traverse City Record-Eagle*." He pulled out a worn newspaper story and handed it to Pete.

Pete scanned the article. It was from four years earlier and the headline read, "War Hero Found Dead." According to the story, Karl Stroud — they used his real name — was found dead in his trailer in the Bay Area Trailer Park on Friday morning. The story went on to say that Stroud was a decorated veteran who had served in Desert Storm and again in the second Iraq war. Police said they were investigating. Suicide was a possibility.

Pete put the story on the bar. "I'm sorry about Buz," he said. He was beginning to think that the wild story Tod had been telling him might have a kernel of truth to it.

"I knew Buz as well as any man alive," Tod said. "Believe me, there was some connection between his death and the case we were working on."

"It's been four years," Pete said. "Has anything more come out to shed light on his death?"

Tod shook his head again. "Nothing satisfactory." He dragged a sleeve across his eyes again. "But as I said, I'm sure that his death had something to do with the Gallanis. Nothing else makes sense." He paused for a moment. "We were getting too close," he said. "And coming on the heels of that meeting with those growers? Obviously, the Gallanis were afraid we'd stumble onto the truth and mess up their scam."

"Did you tell the police all of this?"

"Sure, I told them," Tod said, "but they didn't do anything about it. Same as the cops down in Detroit. Just shrugged it off. Said it looked like suicide."

"How about the widow — what was her name, Singleton? — what did she do?"

"Tod's death spooked everybody. Mary sold out to GMW. Took the money and ran. Moved to the West Coast to live with her sister, I heard."

"That's an amazing story," Pete said.

"Yeah, well, I lost a good friend and the bad guys just skated. Jesus, what time is it?"

Pete waved a hand at the clock behind the bar and said, "Two-forty."

"I've got to get going," he said. "I promised to meet a guy in Glen Arbor about some strange things that have been happening at his store." He looked at Pete. "Say, if you're not doing anything, you want to ride along?"

"Sorry, I can't," Pete replied. "I'm meeting someone in Frankfort for an early dinner."

"You got a card? I may give you a call after I meet with this guy and get the lay of the land. You seem to have pretty good instincts for this type of thing."

Pete felt his pockets. "Gosh, I'm sorry, I don't. I gave the last two to some real estate developers I met with this morning."

"No sweat, I'll get your number from the phone book. I never forget a good Scandihoovian name. Well, until then," he said. He dropped a twenty on the bar, stood and headed for the door. Pete watched him leave. The sound of an engine revved outside the door and soon faded into the distance.

"I noticed old Elbert was bending your ear pretty good," the bartender said as he cleaned the part of the bar where Tod had been sitting.

"Yeah, an amazing story."

"Which one did he tell you?" the bartender asked.

Pete noticed the tell-tale grin on the bartender's face and briefly summarized the story about the grape growers and Tod's suspicions about mob complicity in the death of Buz.

The bartender continued to grin. "That's one of his favorites."

"Something tells me you don't believe him," Pete said.

"He varies that story from time-to-time so I can't say exactly what I believe or don't believe. But did he tell you that Mrs. Singleton got a protective order from the court precluding Elbert from interfering with her contract to sell her vineyard?"

Pete's eyebrows inched up his forehead. "No."

"I didn't think so. How about when Elbert tried to call a meeting of all the independent growers in the area and no one showed up."

Pete had to grin himself. "No, that's not exactly the story he told."

"How about the mob involvement in our wine industry?"

"Yep, he covered that. Said he couldn't figure out the mob's interest, though. Money laundering, possibly."

"Well, the two brothers he accused of being mobsters both graduated from MIT and have one of the biggest tech businesses in Detroit. They do own GMW and did buy Mrs. Singleton's property, but turned it into one of the finest boutique wineries in the area. But you know how those Italians are." He pronounced the name with a long "I" and peered furtively out from under the collar of his shirt that he'd turned up to create a sinister look.

Pete nearly laughed. He didn't view himself as the gullible sort, but that newspaper story....

"I take it Elbert has been through here before," he said.

"God, yes," the bartender replied. "He cruises up and down M-22 like the hero in that old television series."

"Route 66."

"Yeah, that one."

"He claims he's on his way up to Glen Arbor," Pete said. "Said he had to see a guy about some strange goings-on at his store."

"That sounds like Elbert. He doesn't falsify things as much as he twists them. There's always some truth to his stories, but he takes the kernel, and turns it into something sinister that he can investigate."

"That true of Buz, too?" Pete asked.

The bartender looked puzzled. "You mean Karl Stroud?"

"Yeah."

"That's a tragic story. Karl was in and out of the VA hospital for years. He had that posttraumatic thing."

"Posttraumatic stress disorder?"

"Yeah, that's what he had. From the Iraq wars. He rode with Elbert exactly one weekend. I understand the doctors said it probably played to his own fantasies. He finally went off the deep end and killed himself."

Pete just shook his head. "What about his car?" he finally said. "Was that a fabrication, too?"

"No, his car did burn. But the police investigated and concluded that poor old Karl had torched it himself."

THE BURGLAR'S TALE

Charlie Fain wasn't a cold case man. He liked to arrive at the scene of a crime while the blood on the floor was still warm, hook his thumbs in his belt, and take charge from the get-go. Like with the Pavia case or the Bucktown serial murders. Mopping up after other detectives just wasn't his thing.

But that was back when he could be choosy. Before he had to dance to the tune of his new boss, Springdale Police Chief Duane Berens. And the Chief wanted him to take a fresh look at a case that had been cold as the polar ice cap for over two years.

Charlie's sour mood improved when he discovered that the case involved the murder of Karl Rheinfeldt four years earlier. Charlie was working homicide for Chicago PD at the time, but had followed the case in the press out of professional interest. There had been plenty to follow. When a vic's remains had to be power-washed off the driveway of his Tudor mansion, the media vultures had a predictable feeding frenzy.

Two weeks into his "fresh look," Charlie arrived at the municipal building for a meeting with the Chief and a former detective who'd been involved in the investigation. He was early and the Chief was in the process of reacquainting himself with the case. The old cop's brows, perched over his eyes like two albino caterpillars, bobbed up and down as he pawed through the file. Periodically he would grunt as something he read struck a note.

"You know," the Chief said, looking up at Charlie, "this is the only major crime we weren't able to solve in my 20 years as Chief."

Charlie nodded and pursed his lips, trying to appear sympathetic. He chose not to point out there had been only two murders in suburban Springdale during that period, and that included the one he'd solved the previous October. "Maybe we'll be able to correct that, Chief," he said. "Give you a perfect record."

The Chief's chuckle came from deep in his gut. "I like that, Fain," he said, "I like that a lot." Then he cocked one eye at Charlie. "I had reservations about hiring you, as I'm sure you know. You're here only as a favor to our friend downtown. But I have to give you your due. You did a helluva job on the Pavia case." He raised his coffee mug. "You want some?"

Charlie politely declined; the thought of ingesting one more sip of the sludge the Chief passed off as coffee caused his stomach to churn. It was nice to hear the compliment, though, even if it was a little backhanded. His goal was to get back to a big time homicide position and keeping the Chief happy was part of the game plan.

The Chief settled in behind his desk again, took a long slurp from his brimming mug, and glanced at his watch. "Tom should be here in 15 minutes," he said. He sorted through a stack of papers and then looked up. One corner of his mouth curled into a little smirk. Charlie had seen that look before and braced himself.

"Now that it's over," the Chief said, "maybe you can be honest with me. You slept with her that afternoon, right?"

The "her" was Angie Pavia, wife of the man who'd been murdered on the day in question. The Chief was a suspicious old bird, and with some justification since he knew Charlie had been run out of the Chicago PD when his afternoon liaisons with a district captain's wife had come to light. Even homicide head Dan Considine, the "friend" to whom the Chief had referred, hadn't been able to save his star protégé's hide after that one.

"No," Charlie said, "I didn't as a matter of fact. Mrs. Pavia just said that to get at me because I nailed her son for the murder."

The Chief's smirk morphed into a full-blown grin. "C'mon, you son of a buck. I won't hold it against you. I owe you for wrapping up that case so fast."

Charlie knew better than to be baited into a stupid admission. And admitting he'd spent the afternoon of the murder at the Frontage Motel with Angie Pavia would elevate stupidity to new heights.

"Chief," he said. "I just told you. I didn't. None of her story checked out."

The Chief kept grinning like a man who'd just run the table in a game of eight-ball with his best friend. "Okay," he said, waving a meaty paw at Charlie, "we'll talk about it over a beer sometime." He shuffled more papers and then said, "Before Tom gets here, what's your take on the Rheinfeldt case?"

Charlie pounced on the opportunity to shift the conversation to safer ground. "It certainly didn't go unsolved for lack of firepower," he said, smiling. "You had, what, two detectives from the department on it full time? The FBI was involved. There were forensics people from the state. Folks from the task force."

"We had people up the ying yang," the Chief said. "And they came up empty. Nothing. Nada."

Charlie ran a hand through his unruly dark hair. "Your lead detective on the case, Paul Johnson, he's dead, right?"

"Died last year," the Chief said, gazing out the window with a faraway look in his eyes. "Retired after 30 years on the force and moved to a golf community in Florida." He paused. "Never should have retired, I guess."

Charlie shook his head and joined the Chief in admiring the snow-covered pines outside the window as he reflected on the fortunes of life. "What's Tom Crimmons like?" he asked after a few moments.

The Chief idly drummed the end of his Bic pen on the file jacket. "Pretty good detective. He really ran the Rheinfeldt case for us because Paul's head was already in Florida. Not very sociable. Never showed up at department functions where spouses or dates were invited."

"He married?"

"Wasn't when he left the department," the Chief said. "Young guy, early thirties. The Rheinfeldt case seemed to change him. Just up and quit two years ago"

"What's he do now?" Charlie asked.

"Runs some electronics store south of town." The Chief continued the ratatat with his pen. "I've been meaning to go see his place, but just haven't gotten around to it."

Crimmons arrived 20 minutes late. At six-feet plus himself, Charlie didn't look up at many people, but he got the feeling he'd wind up with a stiff neck if he had to stand and talk to Tom Crimmons for more than a few minutes. The guy had to be six-five or six-six. And so reed thin he was at risk of being blown right off the street by a wintry gust. Charlie had made his annual New Year's resolution to shed a few pounds, but looking at Crimmons, he wondered if he should abandon the idea just out of an abundance of caution.

"I know it's been a while," Charlie said after the usual social pleasantries, "but I'm interested in your perspective on the case. You know, looking back after a couple of years."

Crimmons declined the Chief's offer of coffee, which Charlie thought showed good judgment, and then said, "Sure, anything I can do to help. My opinion hasn't changed, though."

"You're convinced it was a mob hit I understand."

Crimmons nodded.

"You care to elaborate?" Charlie said when Crimmons didn't volunteer any details.

The former detective shrugged. "Not much to elaborate on. Karl Rheinfeldt was known to associate with mob figures. We thought they might have been silent partners in his contracting business, or maybe he was laundering money for them. Rheinfeldt probably got crossways with them for some reason."

"Any evidence of a mob connection in his accounting records?"

Crimmons shook his head. "We brought in a forensic accountant, but he didn't find anything." Then he added, "I don't know how much experience you've had with organized crime, but those guys don't exactly leave a nice little roadmap for you to follow."

Charlie ignored the cheap shot from Crimmons and said dryly, "Well, I guess we all agree with that."

Crimmons' account of the crime was consistent with what was in the file. The Chief had sent Johnson and Crimmons to the Rheinfeldt home shortly after the call came in from a neighbor about nine that morning. The fire department, some paramedics and two uniformed officers were already there when they arrived. After securing the crime scene, they conducted preliminary interviews with some of the neighbors and learned that the vic's Cadillac Escalade had been seen parked in his driveway early that morning. They concluded that the vehicle had been left out overnight and that's when the bomb had been rigged.

"No one else was home, right?" Charlie asked.

Crimmons shot the Chief a look that suggested he thought Charlie might have a learning disability. "That's right," he said, "just like the report says. The vic's wife was at a spa in California."

Charlie again ignored the sarcasm. "Did you regard her as a suspect? It wouldn't be the first time a woman wanted her husband out of the way for some reason."

"She certainly was a person of interest," Crimmons said, "but we crossed her off as a suspect, and for good reason. Her alibi checked out, and there was no evidence of motive on her part. No marital problems or anything."

After Crimmons had left, Charlie turned to the Chief. "Is he always that prickly?"

The Chief waved one of his big paws. "He's just defensive. Probably thinks you're trying to second guess him and the other law enforcement officials involved in the case."

Charlie nodded. "He's clearly stuck on the organized crime angle. But you know, after poking around, I haven't found any indication the mob was behind Rheinfeldt's death. There's nothing on the street to that effect. My snitches don't believe Rheinfeldt was involved in mob business, either. They say he was just one of those guys who liked to hobnob with some goodfellas now and then."

"Interesting," the Chief said. He was staring out the window again. "Jesus, I barely recognized Tom. I bet he's down another 20 pounds since he left the department and he'd been losing weight while he was with us"

"I wonder what his secret is," Charlie said, patting his midsection.

"Don't know," the Chief replied. "But he looks like crap."

■ ■ ■

Charlie's background check on Karl Rheinfeldt confirmed that he had been known to socialize with reputed mob figures, but there was nothing tying him to any illegal activities. The only blemish on his record was a fatal automobile accident seven years earlier. Rheinfeldt had claimed that the other driver, a young school teacher named Carla Manning, ran a stop sign and that he'd been unable to stop in time. She died after being in a coma for a month. Rheinfeldt received a suspended sentence as part of a plea agreement.

"I remember the accident," the Chief said. "I always thought the guy had been speeding, but the State's Attorney wasn't sure he could make charges stick at trial so he and Rheinfeldt's lawyer cut a deal."

"Do you think the accident might have provided a motive for someone to kill him? Maybe someone in the Manning family?"

The Chief grimaced. "I don't know, Charlie. The accident happened, what, three years before Rheinfeldt was murdered?"

Charlie nodded. "Here's something else, then. I managed to get the telephone records of the California spa where Mrs. Rheinfeldt was staying. They show she made three calls back to this area the day before the murder. One was to the Rheinfeldt home and the others were to a number we haven't been able to trace yet."

The Chief's eyes widened. "You raised that when Crimmons was here. You suggesting Mrs. Rheinfeldt might have arranged a hit on her husband and set herself up with a nice alibi?"

"Possible," Charlie said, shrugging. "I understand she took up with some other guy not long after the murder. She's apparently a big shopper, too. Maybe there was more conflict between the Rheinfeldts than we think. None of this seems to have been checked out."

The Chief had that faraway look in his eyes again. "A lot of it was the FBI," he said. "They got involved because everyone assumed the murder was tied to organized crime. The case just kind of withered when they weren't able to pin anything on the mob. That's why I asked you to take a fresh look." The Chief paused for a moment and then his face crinkled into a grin. "But I don't want you taking up with Mrs. Rheinfeldt."

Charlie deliberately widened his eyes, like he'd been caught. "Matter of fact," he said, "I've already spent some time with her."

The Chief's massive brows jerked halfway up his forehead. "You didn't...."

Charlie quickly held up a hand in defense. "Don't worry, Chief," he said, "it was strictly business. Besides, she might turn out to be the black widow. You think I'd take a chance with someone like that?"

The Chief scowled. "Well you keep your zipper up while you're working for me."

"You have my word," Charlie said. They sat quietly for a minute or two, each alone with his thoughts. Then Charlie broke the silence. "You know, something else about this case bothers me."

The Chief looked at him. "Yeah? What's that?"

"The way Rheinfeldt was killed. It was a very powerful charge. There are lots of ways to kill a man, but this one strikes me as either intended to send a message or to give vent to some real hate."

"Your message point would fit with the mob hit theory," the Chief said thoughtfully.

"It would," Charlie replied. "But how about hate? That would fit, too."

The Chief nodded and formed his thick hands into a steeple. "I suppose it might. Maybe something real personal was behind it," he said. "Like you suggested, maybe someone in the Manning family couldn't get over Carla's death and decided to extract a pound of flesh."

"Right," Charlie said. "Turning Rheinfeldt into a blob of grease in his own vehicle might have been regarded as..."

"Poetic justice," the Chief said. He spat out the words and looked like a man who'd just had an epiphany.

"Yeah, poetic justice."

The Chief shook his head. "You're good. I can see why Considine was sorry to lose you."

Charlie smiled. "Well, I'm going to put out some feelers on the guy Mrs. Rheinfeldt was seeing and then bounce these things off Tom Crimmons."

"You didn't tell Crimmons you planned to talk to him again."

"No," Charlie said, "I didn't. I thought I'd surprise him and see how he reacts to my latest round of second guessing."

■ ■ ■

Pouring over high school yearbooks for two hours had put Charlie in a pensive mood. And made him think of Sandra Stickl from his own school days. When she'd moved to Wyoming with her family after sophomore year, he felt like he'd been dealt a mortal blow. For months he would close his eyes and imagine her in a fringed buckskin jacket and her favorite designer jeans, cantering across the prairie on an Appaloosa, honey-blonde hair floating in the breeze. He'd fantasized about coming to her rescue just as some low-life was about to do her wrong. He sighed. Ah, the passion of young love.

Charlie shook himself back to reality when he reached the electronics store. A frown crept over Tom Crimmons' face when Charlie walked in, and he made a show of talking to customers for the next 20 minutes.

"You think of more questions you'd rather ask me instead of reading the file?" he said when he finally came over to where Charlie stood.

Charlie smiled. "I've uncovered some things about the case," he said. "I'd like to bounce them off you if you have a few minutes."

Crimmons stared at him. "Really. What kind of things?"

Charlie jerked his head in the direction of a couple who seemed interested in their conversation and said, "Is there somewhere we can talk in private?"

After hesitating for a moment, Crimmons told his customers he'd be right back and then led Charlie into a back office. Stacks of invoices and other papers littered the cramped space. The only personal effects were framed photographs of an older couple, probably his parents, and of a dark haired young woman with a smile straight from a Colgate ad. Charlie stared at her. The Chief obviously didn't know everything about his former detective's social life.

"So what are these hot developments?" Crimmons asked.

Charlie told him about the calls Janet Rheinfeldt had made from her room at the spa the day before the murder. He also mentioned the new man who'd popped up in her life not long after that and how the guy had some shady connections. Then he described his visit to the Mannings and floated his theory about how a family member might have decided to avenge Carla's death.

Crimmons gave him a long look. "I think you're on the wrong track with the Mannings, There was no evidence they were involved. I don't think Mrs. Rheinfeldt was either, but taking a look at the boyfriend might be worth a shot."

"You're probably right about the Mannings," Charlie said. "It was a long time between Carla's accident and when Rheinfeldt was murdered. But I saw hate in her father's eyes. And I understand her older brother had at least one assault charge against him."

Crimmons shrugged. "That doesn't prove anything. You'd feel hate too if something like that happened to your daughter.

And her brother doesn't even live in the area and didn't at the time."

"Well, it's only a theory," Charlie said, "but hate is a powerful emotion and I do plan to take a closer look at the brother. Same with the boyfriend. I've already put out the word on the street so that it will get back to him."

"I think you should be taking another look at the mob angle, too," Crimmons said. "That's the only thing that makes sense. Maybe the boyfriend was connected."

Charlie nodded and continued to debate whether to raise his last point. He finally decided to go with it.

"Look," he said, "I know you're busy so here's the last thing. One of my best snitches has a book on every low-life in the area. He told me he knows a cat burglar who'd been working Springdale around the time of the murder. The Rheinfeldt house was one of the ones he was casing as a possible target. Apparently he saw a man prowling around the vic's SUV that night. Claims he got a good look at him."

Crimmons grunted. "You believe that? Don't you think someone who was going to rig a car bomb would be careful to do it when no one was around?"

"You'd think so," Charlie said. "But keeping out of sight is what a cat burglar does. And I've confirmed there was a near full moon that night so someone prowling around the SUV would have been visible. I guess I'll know more tomorrow night."

Crimmons' interest picked up. "What's tomorrow night?"

"The cat agreed to meet with me so I can hear his story firsthand."

"Sounds like a wild goose chase," Crimmons said, "but if you go, you might want to take someone with you who knows the case better. What time is the meeting?"

"It's at eight," Charlie said, "but the guy insisted I come alone. He also made me promise not to try to nail him for any of the burglaries. He's afraid of being seen with me in public so we're meeting at his apartment."

"Where?" Crimmons asked. "Maywood? That's where most of the guys who work this area come from."

Charlie fished in his pocket and pulled out a scrap of paper. "Berwyn. Thirteen-twenty Taylor Street, 2B."

"Okay," Crimmons said. "Good luck." He looked back as he opened the office door. "I'm sure you'll let me know if you have more questions."

■ ■ ■

Charlie thought about having a snort or two from the flask he kept under the passenger seat. Maybe even go home and check directory assistance in Wyoming to see if Sandra was listed. But he got a grip on himself and put his urge for a little diversion aside.

He stopped at a 7-Eleven to stock up on Diet Cokes, the kind with caffeine, and headed for Berwyn. The meeting he'd mentioned to Crimmons wasn't supposed to take place until the following night, but he'd learned over the years that being a little early never hurt. Besides, he had a hunch.

The vestibule of the run-down building at 1320 Taylor listed only unit numbers and no names; Charlie suspected the occupants liked it that way. The second floor hall light was burned out, adding to the seedy look. The worn hardwood floor creaked with each step. As he fished in his pocket for the key, he could smell the odor of stale pizza coming from 2G. No one was home, which he already knew. Dirty dishes and half-empty take-out boxes littered the efficiency kitchen. He appreciated Miguel letting him use the apartment, but would have to lecture him about his housekeeping.

Charlie flicked off the lights and let his eyes grow accustomed to the darkness. The only illumination came through the living room window as a neon sign on the cocktail lounge across the street blinked on and off. Charlie settled down on a couch that looked like it had come from the Salvation Army's reject pile, and placed his Smith & Wesson semiautomatic on the cushion beside him.

After popping a Diet Coke, Charlie reflected on what the night might bring. Certainly, he had enough bait out on the street. The rash of burglaries around the time of Rheinfeldt's murder was convenient, too. Charlie smiled. Burglars might be the scourge of society, but sometimes they could serve the cause of justice. Particularly if trotted out at the right time.

Charlie checked his watch. He'd been there almost two hours. He was about to eat another granola bar when he heard the hall floor creak. He sat motionless and listened. The floor creaked again, this time right outside the apartment door. Charlie grabbed his Smith & Wesson and clicked off the safety. Then he moved quietly across the room, feeling thankful for the carpet, and flattened himself against the wall behind the door.

Someone was fussing with the lock! The light rasp of metal on metal was all that disturbed the silence. Thirty seconds passed. A minute, although it seemed longer. Charlie waited, barely breathing.

The door inched open and a dark-clad figure slid through the crack, moving slowly and without sound, like some enormously elongated cat. Flashes of light through the window intermittently illuminated the man's features not covered by his skull cap.

A jumble of images flashed through Charlie's mind. The photograph in Tom Crimmons' office. Carla Manning in the yearbook dancing cheek-to-cheek with her tall prom escort and sitting moon-eyed at a basketball game as the same young man swished a fifteen-footer over a shorter player. The Chief's comment about poetic justice.

Charlie pointed his Smith & Wesson at the man's thin upper body and said, "I thought you might come, Tom. I'm truly sorry for your loss, but it's over."

LEIF ERIKSON'S GHOST

hunk!

The arrow caught the shoulder of the figure that was barely visible among the trees in the fading light. *Thunk!*

Another arrow found the figure, more toward the middle of his frame this time. The figure shuddered under the impact and fell backward behind a bush.

Pete Thorsen walked over and righted the army surplus target. When he returned, he had a look of satisfaction on his face. "Want to try?" he asked, as he offered the bow to his friend, Harry McTigue.

Harry took the bow and plucked at the string gingerly, as though fearful it would suddenly go berserk and begin to launch arrows in all directions.

"This thing's too long for me," he said, looking at the five-foot bow made of polished yew wood. "I'm used to a bow that's better scaled to the human body. Plus, this light is not good right now."

Pete goaded him with a little grin. "There's still plenty of light. Give it a try."

Harry, apparently noticing Pete's demeanor, gripped the bow and pulled back the string with his right hand. When he got halfway back, Pete saw his arms shake and suppressed the urge to laugh. The pull weight was heavy even for him. Harry returned the string to its normal position, nocked an arrow and pulled back again. The arrow swayed away from the bow as he stood there, no doubt wishing he had three hands. Harry eased the string back again and looked puzzled.

Pete had difficulty stifling his mirth by now and said, "Here," and placed Harry's left hand in the proper position to guide the arrow and stepped back.

With his hand firmly on the grip, Harry started to pull the string back again. He made it less than half way this time. He let go and the arrow flew weakly through the air like a wounded Mallard and struck the ground 20 feet in front of the silhouette target.

Harry stared at his handiwork for a minute, then reached for another arrow. Same awkward form. Same result.

As he watched, Pete was about to stuff a handful of dry leaves in his mouth to avoid laughing.

"I'm just not used to this bow," Harry said thoughtfully. "I was drilling everything dead center when I was out with Lynn." He looked at Pete. "With this light, I guess you have to adjust for distance, too, huh?"

Pete shrugged as he slowly regained his composure. "You said Lynn taught you everything she knew."

"She's a damned good teacher, I'll tell you that. My shot pattern wasn't as tight as hers that day, but I was on target just about every time."

Lynn was Lynn Hawke, Harry's accountant and Pete's love interest until she moved to Seattle to care for her suicidal daughter. She was also a world-class archer and had been an alternate on the U.S. Olympic team 10 years earlier. Pete had practiced with her a couple of times himself. There was no question she was good. Her teaching skills must have been sorely tested when she worked with Harry, though.

"Warm today," Harry said, as he doffed his red fleece vest. His elliptical body strained at his shirt as he swung his right arm in a circular motion to ease his shoulder muscles.

"Indian summer. Supposed to be like this for the next couple of weeks."

Harry looked at Pete as though he were part of his archery problem. "I know you claim to have Viking blood in your veins and you just had that bow made for you in Norway, but if you're going to be a serious archer, you should get yourself fixed up with a more up-to-date bow."

"What do you mean?" Pete asked. "Man has never come up with material for a bow that's superior to the wood of a yew tree. Even Lynn said that."

Harry grunted. "Then why, may I ask, does she have equipment made from that compound stuff or whatever they call it?"

"Fashion," Pete said. "But fashion doesn't mean something is better."

Harry shook his head in disgust. Then he looked at Pete again. "You know, I thought that guy Olf who made that bow was a little off."

"Ulf."

"What?"

"His name is Ulf."

"Whatever," Harry said. "I thought he was a little daffy."

"I beg to differ. You know, he traces his lineage back to Erik the Red."

Harry frowned. "Who's that?"

"A famous Viking who settled Iceland and Greenland."

The disgust on Harry's face was evident. "Both garden spots," Harry said, snorting. "Anyway, so what if Olf can trace his lineage back to this Red guy?"

"C'mon, Harry. How many people do you know who can trace his ancestors back over a thousand years?"

"And who, may I ask, really cares? When you go to the Great Bone Yard in the sky, you suppose the gatekeeper is going to ask whether you were related to Red or Bluebeard or one of those other yokels?"

"I don't know," Pete answered, eyeing him skeptically. "It's kind of nice to know who your ancestors were." He studied his old friend. There were few things he enjoyed more than to get Harry going. "Take you and me," he continued, looking at him knowingly, "if you knew your genealogy, you might discover we're related."

Harry looked at him as if he were as loony as old Ulf. "Huh? We're not related," he said disdainfully. "Your people hung around those fjords and mine came from the highlands where they developed civilized stuff like Scotch."

"You don't know your history, my friend. Who do you think those seafaring people were who came to visit your homeland from time-to-time?"

"Aw, you aren't going to get into that stuff again, are you? Everybody knows that the old Vikings were just a bunch of pirates."

"I tell you, Harry," Pete persisted, "we could be related. We should get together some time and compare our genealogies."

Harry leveled a baleful look at Pete. "Umm, hmm. You don't even know for sure that this Erik guy ever left the fjord country."

"I sure do. It's all in the Icelandic sagas. Erik the Red's family left Norway and he spent his life exploring the north Atlantic. He could have taken a trip or two to Scotland."

"Icelandic sagas. What are those?"

"Recorded history, Harry, recorded history."

"And what do these sagas say about why Erik's family left Norway? You're always telling me it's such a great place. I didn't think it was so great when we were there."

Pete knew he'd worked himself into a corner. Maybe if he got Harry distracted. "We just hit a patch of bad weather."

"Yeah, sure. Well, why did they leave?"

Harry could be annoyingly persistent at times. "I don't remember all of the details," Pete said evasively. "Something about some kind of charges against Erik's father."

Harry looked at him with renewed interest. "Charges. What kind of charges?"

"I'm not sure," Pete said. "The sagas said something about manslaughter."

"Hah! I knew it! Like I said, a bunch of pirates and murderers!"

"Maybe some of them were a little rough around the edges, but they still could have gotten cozy with a few of your women," Pete said.

"Oh, sure," Harry replied dryly. "Nice gentile Scottish women and a bunch of ax murderers. That really sounds probable."

Pete picked up his bow and drilled three arrows in succession into the target. He looked at Harry with a little smirk. "See? It's hereditary."

"Trained killers, that's all," Harry said. "It runs in your blood. By the way, how does that fellow Leif Erikson you're always talking about fit into all of this? I seem to remember you insulting that Italian partner of yours when you were still working."

Pete thought for a minute. "Oh, you mean Mike Scapaletto?"

"That sounds like the guy."

"He didn't like it when I hung a big Norwegian flag outside my office every Columbus Day."

Harry shook his head in disgust. "No respect for one of the nation's most revered holidays." He peered at Pete over his half-glasses. "Didn't you used to send something around to all the people in your firm every Leif Erikson Day, too."

Pete grinned. "Just trying to set the record straight about who was here first. How does Leif Erikson fit in? He was one of Erik the Red's sons and a world-class explorer in his own right. He was the first European to set foot on what is now known as North America."

"That in those sagas, too?

"The sagas and other sources. Historians now pretty much agree that Leif and his party were the first to reach the American continent."

"How many people in that party of his?"

"Don't know for sure, but his father Erik the Red wasn't one of them. Leif invited Erik to go on the voyage, but he fell off his horse and injured himself on the way to the ship. He took that as an omen and bowed out of the trip."

"Besides being a murderer, he couldn't sit a horse, either, huh?" Harry observed with another disdainful look.

"Anyway," Pete said, "Leif and the others went and landed on a place they called Vinland. That's probably Newfoundland these days."

"How far inland did they go?"

"No one knows for sure. They could have made it all the way to northwest Michigan for all we know."

"Oh, sure," Harry said with a snort. "They probably built the Grand Hotel on Mackinac Island, too."

Pete ignored Harry's sarcasm and said, "One final bit of trivia for you. In honor of his father, Leif dyed the feathers on his arrows bright red. A nice touch, huh?"

Harry got a nostalgic look in his eyes. "That is nice," he said. "Honor thy father even if he was an ax murderer. How many kids would do that today?"

Pete smiled and said, "What time are we leaving in the morning?"

"How about six?" Harry replied. "That'll give us time to get to the river, get set up, and be out fishing by eight."

■ ■ ■

It was 7:15 when Pete and Harry reached the access point for their Boardman River fishing outing. As usual, Harry was fully decked out when he picked Pete up. Pete was always fascinated by Harry's fishing vest. It seemed to hold every dry fly known to the angling world and he donned it as soon as he got out of the shower. Put him in the zone, he said. While Pete was donning his own gear, Harry was busy slipping into his waders.

Everything was proceeding on schedule. Harry was habitually late in everything else he did in life. But when it came to fishing, the boys in Greenwich, England could have calibrated their time pieces according to his movements. The guide was there with their canoe, too, and would ferry Harry's SUV down to the Boardman Dam access point where they would wrap up their outing and make the exchange again. Pete and Harry would float down the river until they came to a likely looking stretch of fishing water, work the stream with their fly equipment, and then move on again.

Harry was hot. By his own reckoning, he'd caught nine brook trout and a handful of other species by 9:30. Pete didn't keep track, but knew he wasn't far behind. With catch-and-release, they weren't burdened by the necessity of caring for their catch. It was free-and-easy fishing, the kind both of them enjoyed.

They were back in their canoe and rounding a bend coming up on Scheck's Place Campground when they noticed two uniformed police at the access point, waving at them to pull in. Harry swiveled his head and said, "You got our licenses?" Pete nodded and guided the canoe toward the landing.

"You gentlemen see anyone on the river this morning?" asked one of the officers as they neared shore.

"Not a soul," Harry said. "Fishing's damn good, though."

"You got cell phones with you?"

"Yeah, both of us do."

"Well, if you see anyone — along the shore or on the river — call this number right away." He handed Harry a card. "Don't try to engage them in conversation. Just call and stay clear of them."

Pete and Harry exchanged glances. "You mind telling us what's going on?" asked Pete.

"There's been an incident," one of the officers said. "We're looking for two men. They should be considered very dangerous."

The comment piqued Pete's curiosity. "What kind of an incident?" he asked. The lawyer in him was taking over. He didn't like half-information.

This time it was the officers' turn to exchange glances. "Someone broke into a house upriver early this morning. There have been three homicides. We have a pretty good idea who did it."

"They killed all the occupants?" Harry asked, beginning to sense a big news story.

"Yes," one of the uniforms replied.

Harry pulled out a small notebook and began to scribble away. "Where did this happen?" he asked, golf pencil poised over the notebook to record the details.

One uniform squinted at him suspiciously. "You a reporter?"

"I own *The Northern Sentinel* over in Frankfort."

"Well, we're not releasing any information to the media yet. Let's just say it happened upriver a ways."

"Can you at least give me a few more details about what happened?" Harry asked.

"Sorry," the officer said, shaking his head.

"How about the family — I assume it was a family, right?" Harry persisted. "Could you confirm that and give me their names?"

"Sorry," the officer replied for the second time, shaking his head again. "Let's just say it was a pretty bad scene."

"Jesus," Harry muttered under his breath. "You think they took to the river to escape, huh?"

"We're not sure. We found an old abandoned pickup back a ways. We've got the roads blocked off and are checking the river just to be sure they didn't follow it out."

"Mmm," Harry murmured.

"Now remember, you seen anyone, you call us immediately. Understood? Don't go off and try to get the story yourself. We'll release the details to the press in due course."

With that final admonition, the two officers turned and walked up the bank toward their cruiser.

Harry looked back at Pete and asked, "Well, what do you think?"

"Sounds like a bad situation, but the police seem to have it well in hand."

Harry hesitated for a moment and then said, "Do you suppose it would be worthwhile for us to backtrack a ways and see if we can find that house?"

"Harry, are you crazy? We're here to fish. We don't know how far back that place is or even whether it's located on the river. Besides, even if we found the house, they've probably got it taped off and the police wouldn't let us near the place."

"I suppose you're right," Harry said, not sounding convinced. "I guess it's the newsman in me coming out. I sure would like to see that house, though, so I could work it into my story."

"Harry...."

"Okay, okay, I was just thinking out loud." He paused. "One more question...what do you think the motivation might have been to kill a whole family?"

"We don't know it was the whole family."

"Sounds like it."

"Who knows what the motivation was," Pete said. "The world is full of psychos these days."

"I guess I'm just more intellectually curious about these things than you are. Maybe that's why I'm a newspaperman."

"Are we going to get back to fishing or what?"

Harry gave Pete a dirty look and used his paddle to push the canoe out in the current. Soon they were floating down-river again. Pete watched his friend with admiration. Harry was one of the least athletic people he knew, but put him around a canoe and he was practically the model of grace.

They floated for a while, occasionally dipping their paddles in the water to slow their passage downstream or to steer the canoe around obstacles. As they drifted along, they both kept an eye on the shore, but tried not to be too obvious about it. The leaves had been late in turning — too much warm weather — and it was difficult to see beyond the shoreline.

When they came to a fruitful looking stretch of the stream, they guided their canoe onto a sandbar and began to cast for trout again. Besides being an accomplished canoe man, Harry was a first-rate fly fisherman and Pete watched him work the river for a few minutes. His split-bamboo rod was the best Orvis had to offer. Harry brought the rod back to eleven o'clock and flicked it forward so the fly attached to his double-taper line landed under an overhanging tree. Artistry in motion.

As Pete was watching, he saw something move in the trees along the river. It was just a flash, and he heard no sound of twigs snapping or other sounds unfamiliar to the forest. Pete strained for a better look. Suddenly he was aware of his companion staring at him.

"I know," Harry whispered when they locked eyes, "I saw it, too."

They stood in the river with the gentle waves lapping at their waders, eyes fixed on the brush on the other side. Suddenly there was another flash through the leaves, a little farther down stream.

"There it is again," Harry whispered hoarsely. "Maybe it was a deer."

Pete shook his head. "That was no deer."

They stood motionless in the water for another few minutes. Finally, Harry said, "I don't hear anything."

Pete nodded his head in agreement

"Do you think we ought to call?" Harry asked softly.

This time Pete nodded. "But let's get back to our canoe first. We're really exposed where we are. Act normal — make a few more casts — and work our way over."

They took turns casting, both anxious to get out of the river. Thankfully, the sandbar where they'd left the canoe was on the opposite side of the river from the flashes they'd both seen in the brush. They reached the canoe and eased it off the sand until it was floating again. They used their paddles to guide the canoe along the side of the river and to slow their natural float downriver. Harry fished out his cell phone and looked at the card the officers had given him. He punched in the numbers and waited a few moments. Then he punched in the numbers again and listened a second time.

"Shit," he said. "No service out here. Want to try?" He handed the card to Pete. He tried to call and didn't get a connection either.

"What should we do?" Harry asked.

"Whatever we saw was headed downriver," Pete said. "I suggest we stay here for an hour or so. The next access point is Brown Bridge Dam. That's four or five miles away. If we make it down there, hopefully we'll be able to get service or there'll be other fishermen around and we can reach our guide and have him come get us."

"Why don't we get going now?"

"Look, if we start now, we're apt to overtake anyone walking along the bank. I don't think that's very smart, do you?"

"I see what you mean."

They found another sandbar and eased the front of the canoe onto it. For the next hour, they sat there by the brush and waited. Finally, Harry turned to Pete and said, "Maybe it's drug-related. I hear there's a lot of drug activity around Traverse City."

"Drugs don't seem like a reason to kill an entire family."

"I don't know, maybe they were trying to send a message."

Just then a twig snapped in the bushes. Pete and Harry both jumped and frantically peered into the brush. A few moments later, a doe came out and began to lap at the water. They breathed sighs of relief. Harry turned back to Pete and asked, "You sure that wasn't a deer back there, too?"

"I tell you, Harry, that was no deer. I caught a flash through the trees. It looked like a man to me. But dressed in some kind of animal skin."

Harry peered at Pete over his glasses for a long time. "You think it was a man then?"

"Looked like it to me. But I'm just telling you what I think I saw."

"I'm ready to get out of here." Harry said. "What time is it?"

"It's been close to an hour. Let's go. But don't rush things."

They let the lazy current carry them downstream again, watching for signs of life along the bank. There were none. They'd gone a couple of miles when Harry pointed to the riverbank and whispered over his shoulder, "What's that?"

Pete peered into the water on the other side of the river. He saw the same thing that Harry saw. "Could be trash," Pete said. He stared at the object some more. "Looks like clothes."

As they drifted closer, Harry swiveled his head and said nervously, "Pete, I think that's a body!"

Pete rummaged through his duffle and pulled out a pair of binoculars. He trained them on the object. "You're right," he said, "it is a body." He got an icy feeling in the pit of his stomach. He scanned the shore and then looked downriver. "Look," he said, "there's another one!"

"Jesus!" Harry said. "Let me see." He reached back for the binoculars, and after adjusting them, focused on the second hulking shape in the water.

After a few moments, he lowered the binoculars and turned to Pete and whispered, "You don't suppose the killers came upon two more people and got them, too?"

Pete just stared at the bodies in the water. "Let me have those glasses again." He sat there for a few minutes, training the binoculars on the object in the water and then scanning the shoreline and the terrain that bordered it. "I don't see anything," he said. "Let's get a little closer."

"You think that's smart?" Harry whispered back.

"You're the one who wanted to go back to that house and witness the carnage."

"Yeah, but that was a secure place. What if the killers are on shore somewhere watching us?"

That thought had occurred to Pete as well. But sitting in a canoe on the side of the river, they were in the open anyway. He tried his cell phone again. Still no connection. "Come on," he said. "Let's get closer. I haven't seen any signs of life on the shore."

"You want to take the front then?"

They scrambled around and switched places. Then they started edging toward the first body.

"This close enough?" Harry whispered.

"A little closer."

"Jesus," Harry muttered again under his breath

As they floated closer to the body, Pete stared at it intensely.

"Any closer," Harry said nervously, "and you'll be able to touch the body with your paddle."

"That's what I want to do," Pete answered. Harry just shook his head and let the canoe drift closer.

When they got within paddle distance, Pete reached out and poked at the body. "Harry," he said, "it looks like this one's got an arrow in him." The body was laying mostly face-down, a little on his side. He repositioned his paddle and gave a shove. The arrow came into view. He eased back on the paddle and the body returned to its former face-down position in the water.

"I'll bet the other body has an arrow in it, too," Pete said. Harry just continued to stare.

Pete tried his cell phone again and this time his call connected. When the person at the other end answered, he identified himself and said, "We're a couple of miles south of Brown Bridge Dam. There are two more bodies in the river. You better get your people over here as soon as possible."

When he got off the phone, Harry was still staring intently at the body in the water. Occasionally he glanced at the brush along the shore, then his eyes returned to the body.

Pete turned back to him and asked, "Did you see that arrow when I pushed the body?"

Harry didn't answer for a long time. Then he nodded and said softly, "Red feathers."

OPENING DAY

us Minetti was thinking murder. He'd just gotten off the phone with Harry McTigue who'd updated him on the trial in which Harry and Pete Thorsen had been called to testify. The defendant in the case was a man named Joseph Stenerud, known to everyone in the community in which he lived as "Old Joe."

"Not the same without Harry and Pete here," Herb Baxter said wistfully. They were sitting at their usual table at Elsie's Roadhouse enjoying smoked whitefish pate while waiting for their dinner. Trout season had opened that morning, and eating at Elsie's had become a tradition. For the past seven years, there'd always been four of them; this year there were two.

"No, it's not the same," Gus said thoughtfully. Then he added, "According to Harry, the prosecution is still putting on their case. Harry and Pete expect to testify tomorrow. I don't know whether they'll have to hang around, but if they join us, it'll only be for the last day."

Old Joe lived along the banks of the Boardman River, south of Traverse City. He was known as an eccentric and could often be seen working out on an elaborate outdoor facility he'd built of treated logs. During bow season, the old Viking in him came out and he often dressed in animal skins and could be seen skulking through the woods. A dangerous habit, to say the least. About the only person he ever talked to was Dorothy Pauling who lived across the road from his shack. When two crack-heads murdered the entire Pauling family one morning, Old Joe was accused of tracking them down and killing both of them with arrows to the chest. The red-feathered arrows were the tip-off for the authorities. He was known to favor the arrows which, according to legend, were used by Leif Erikson as a tribute to his father. Pete and Harry found the bodies in the river while fishing one day.

Besides missing his fishing companions, Gus had something on his mind other than the trial. Early that morning, as he and Herb were cutting through the woods to the trout stream, they'd seen a man digging outside his home and thought it was a little strange. Try as he might, he couldn't get out of his mind questions about why a man would be out digging that early. The old detective in him smelled something.

The only thing Herb smelled was the food. He'd just polished off his first serving of one of Elsie's famous pot roast dinners, and shamelessly held out his plate for seconds. When Harry McTigue was with them, it was always a contest to see which of them could put away more of Elsie's home cooking. While Herb was chewing, Gus saw him eye the cherry pies on the counter. Pies made the right way, without that flaky crust nonsense.

Elsie hovered near their table like a loving mother fawning over two favorite sons. Her trademark flaming tresses, courtesy of Clairol, framed a gentle face that, as always, looked freshly scrubbed.

She beamed as Herb commenced his assault on the pie. Then a hint of sadness crept into her eyes. "I miss not seeing Harry and Pete."

"Testifying at that trial I told you about," Herb mumbled with his mouth full of pie. "They'll be back next year. I'm planning a five-day trip for us. You'll get tired of seeing us."

Elsie turned her gaze to Gus who'd been quiet most of the evening. "You're awfully quiet, Gus," she said. Then she added, "You miss it, don't you?"

Gus took his time savoring a bite of pie. "Miss what?" he asked after swallowing.

"You know," she said, "the detective work."

Gus grunted. "Why would I miss it? It's kind of nice to spend my time with normal people instead of dealing with a bunch of scum." Then a smirk tugged at one corners of his mouth. "Not that Herb is all that normal."

Herb shot him a look and jabbed the air with his fork. "Oh, no, he don't miss it," he said as he scraped his plate to capture the last morsel of pie. "He only calls me about eight times a day to complain about how some case is being mishandled. And he's been on the phone with Harry constantly looking for updates on the trial and offering his opinions on the case."

The mishandling comment must have struck a cord because he said, somewhat indignantly, "Well, it's true. Prosecutors are all political these days, and the police screw up cases left and right."

Herb rolled his eyes and eyed the pie tin Elsie had moved within reach.

The truth was that Gus did miss it. Twenty-six years as a homicide detective couldn't be swept aside just like that even if he once thought it could. He had no hobbies except fly fishing, and his wife had settled into her own routine and wasn't too interested in changing at this point in her life. He'd gotten his private investigator's license to keep his hand in, but marital infidelity and insurance fraud cases didn't exactly get his juices flowing.

"Elsie," Gus said, as his eyes idly swept the familiar knotty pine walls adorned with trophy trout specimens, "what do you know about that guy who lives down by the river?"

She frowned. "You mean Karl Meier?"

"I don't know his name. He lives in that log house up on the bluff. What do you know about him?"

"That's Mr. Meier. I don't know much about him, really. He was never very sociable, and he's even worse since he lost his wife."

Herb slid another wedge of pie from the tin. Without looking up from his primary interest of the moment, he said, "That's the guy whose wife ran off on him, right?"

"Yes, it was very sad."

"What happened?" Gus asked.

"No one knows for sure," Elsie said. "Her and Mr. Jemkow disappeared on the same day and no one ever heard from them again. I guess Mr. Meier took it real hard."

Gus ran a hand through his thick gray-flecked hair and swung his chair around to stretch his legs. He attributed his stiffness to sitting around the house too much and not getting out on the streets.

"Were the Meiers having marital problems?" he asked.

Elsie pursed her lips and shrugged. "Everyone thought they had a loving relationship. They both loved to fish and people would see them down by the river together all the time."

"Who was this Jemkow guy?" Herb asked.

"Mr. Jemkow was new to these parts. Seemed like a nice man and everything. Mr. Meier reported Alice missing and then they discovered that Mr. Jemkow was missing, too. That was over three years ago."

Gus nodded. "So the assumption was they ran off together."

"Yes," Elsie said. "Mr. Jemkow's car was gone, and all of his clothes. The both of them just vanished."

"Any signs they'd been having an affair?"

"Some people thought so," Elsie said. "The hardware store man said he was fishing once and was sure he saw them up on the river bank sitting real close." She paused. "I think they first met when Mr. Jemkow did some repair work on the Meier's roof. That's how he made a living, doing odd jobs for people."

Gus mulled over what Elsie had just told them and stared at an impressive brook trout mounted on a weathered piece of wood over the bar. It had been his contribution to the restaurant's decor.

Herb sat quietly and tried to be inconspicuous as he loosened his belt a notch. He glanced at the pie, but didn't reach for the tin again.

"Why are you so interested in Mr. Meier, Gus?"

Herb snorted. "He's playing detective again," he said before Gus could answer. "I told you, he can't get it out of his system."

Gus ignored the zinger and said, "You know how Herb and I like to get down to the river early? We always cut through the woods near the Meier place. This morning someone — I assume it was Karl Meier — was out digging about six. That strike you as odd?"

Herb grinned. "Gus thinks Meier might be a serial murderer and was burying some bodies."

"I don't necessarily think he's a serial murderer," Gus said, "but you have to admit it's pretty damned unusual. In April, it's not like you have to start work early to beat the heat. Last year on opening day he was out digging early, too. I didn't think much about it at the time, but two years in a row and it kind of grabs your attention."

Elsie and Herb just stared at him, as though at a loss for words.

Gus didn't say anything about what bothered him the most. He was pretty sure he'd seen a box of some sort near where Meier had been digging. Maybe, Gus thought, he should have a closer look at the dig site on their way to the river the next morning.

■ ■ ■

Gus received a cool reception from the Sheriff when he suggested a search of the Meier property. Lack of probable cause and all that stuff, the Sheriff said. But the Sheriff didn't require a lot of persuading to go along with an alternative Gus laid out. The reason was simple enough. Gus's plan would provide the Sheriff deniability if necessary yet allow him to claim credit if it resulted in solving the mysterious disappearances of two of the county's citizens. The perfect scenario for a politically ambitious man.

The following day, after another good morning of catch-and-release, they called on Karl Meier. Herb wasn't too keen on the idea, but Gus had convinced him that worst case they might be treated rudely and asked to leave.

"Mr. Meier," Gus said when a man answered his knock, "my name is Gus Minetti. I'm a private investigator." He flashed his credentials. "This is my colleague, Herb Baxter," he added, gesturing toward Herb who'd remained at the bottom of the porch steps.

Meier, a wiry man with a pinched, humorless face, stared at Gus through the partially open door. He ignored Gus's outstretched hand.

"Can't you read, Mister?" he finally said. "Them signs say no trespassing."

"Listen, Mr. Meier, I'm not trespassing. I've just come to ask you a few questions. Some dogs have disappeared recently, and a couple of families have hired me to investigate. I'm talking to everyone in the area."

As he spoke, Gus could see Herb roll his eyes at the missing dog explanation and begin to fidget.

Karl Meier's thin lips tightened. "I ain't heard nothin' about no missing dogs," he said, spitting out the words like a mouthful of bitter seeds. "Now I'm asking you to leave."

"There's no reason to get upset," Gus said. "All I need is five minutes of your time. By the way, you building something over there? I noticed the digging." Gus gestured toward the fresh dirt.

Meier's eyes flicked in the direction Gus had pointed. Color rose in his weathered face and his jaw tensed. "By God, I've had enough of this!" He whirled and went back into the house.

"Jesus, Gus," Herb said, "let's get out of here. The guy's nuts."

Gus looked at him. He was forced to admit that he hadn't expected such a hostile reception. He'd encountered a lot of that in his former line of work, but then he'd had the comfort of a badge and, more importantly, his Smith & Wesson. Herb was right, too; the guy did seem nuts.

As Gus thought about what to do, Meier kicked open the door and emerged with an over-under shotgun clutched in his hands. "You got five seconds to get off my property, Mister, or they'll have to carry you off!"

Gus moved back down the porch steps, eyeing the business end of Meier's shotgun. The barrels looked the size of two drainage pipes. A sick feeling clutched his stomach, like he'd been kicked in the crotch. Where the hell was the Sheriff? Had something gone wrong? Then, just as he was about to retreat down the gravel road, the Sheriff trotted out of the woods with a fresh-faced Deputy in tow.

"What's going on, here?" he called in a gruff voice. "I heard the ruckus way down by the river."

Meier stood on the porch with a surprised look on his hatchet face. His shotgun remained pointed at Gus's midsection.

"Mr. Meier," the Sheriff said as he got closer, "you'd best put that weapon down before someone gets hurt." His right hand rested on his holstered side arm.

Meier looked down at the shotgun in his hands and then at the Sheriff. "These guys was trespassing on my property," he finally said. "I'm just protecting my rights."

"Okay, okay," the Sheriff said in a soothing voice. "But you need to put that shotgun down so we can talk about it. It's Karl, isn't it? You don't want assault with a deadly weapon charges against you, Karl. That's real serious."

Gus exhaled slowly as Meier, appearing confused, lowered the shotgun and leaned it against the porch rail.

"Now," the Sheriff said, shifting his gaze to Gus and Herb, "why don't you fellows introduce yourselves and explain what you're doing on Mr. Meier's property."

"I'm Gus Minetti. I'm a private investigator. This is my colleague, Herb Baxter. We're looking into the missing dog problem and just wanted to ask Mr. Meier a few questions."

The Sheriff nodded and motioned for Meier to come down the steps to join them. "You know anything about these missing dogs, Karl?"

"Like I told these yahoos, I don't know nothin' about no missing dogs. Now get them off my property, Sheriff, before I grab my Remington and finish the job."

The Sheriff held up a hand, palm out. "Just stay calm, Karl. Mr. Minetti," he continued, looking at Gus, "what makes you think Mr. Meier here knows anything about these dogs?"

Gus could tell from the Sheriff's demeanor that his resolve for seeing their plan through might be wavering. He played his trump card.

"For one thing, we saw Mr. Meier burying something over there." Gus pointed in the direction of the fresh earth. "It could be one of the dogs. He was seen digging last year, too, when a couple of dogs were reported missing."

Meier's face became flushed again and he took a step toward Gus. "There ain't no dogs buried over there, you sonofabitch!"

"Whoa, whoa," the Sheriff said. "We need to talk this thing through, like I said."

Good, Gus thought, the Sheriff had been propped, at least for the moment. It was time to press his advantage.

"Ask him what's buried over there, then," Gus said to the Sheriff.

"It ain't none of your goddamned business!" Meier screamed. He started toward Gus again.

"Karl," the Sheriff said, stepping in his way, "I'm not going to warn you again. You need to keep yourself under control. Now why don't you tell us what you've got buried under that fresh dirt."

Meier stared at the ground. "It's private," he muttered. "Ain't nobody's business but mine."

"Well, I can't say I agree with you, Karl. It looks like it could be a public matter. Since you won't cooperate, by the authority vested in me as the Sheriff of this county, I'm ordering that area over there with the fresh dirt be excavated. Sam," he said to his Deputy, "get a shovel."

Gus tried not to grin. So much for probable cause and search warrants. It was clear the Sheriff wanted to see what was buried in the ground and he wanted to see it now. Hopefully a good prosecutor would be able to repair any damage if they were to find something.

Sam attacked his excavation chores with energy, although his facial expression suggested resentment over being required to perform menial labor like some grunt infantryman digging in for the night. The dirt flew off his shovel and soon he was thigh-deep in the hole.

"Hey!" the Deputy called. "I think I found something!"

Karl Meier's eyes flicked toward the hole ever so briefly and then he resumed staring at the ground. The others crowded around the hole, straining for a better look, as Sam continued to dig. Ten minutes later he had scraped the dirt off the top of what appeared to be a wooden box. Gus and the Sheriff helped him hoist the box to the surface. It was in the size and shape of a child's coffin.

The Sheriff walked over to the porch rail and moved the shotgun farther away from Meier. Then he looked at him and said, "You want to tell us what's in the box, Karl?"

Meier's sullen expression didn't change. "I told you," he mumbled without looking up, "it's private."

"Okay, Sam," the Sheriff said, "open 'er up."

The Deputy pried open the box with the tip of his shovel and flung back the lid. A fly rod and reel, broken down and protected by a plastic sheath, lay on top of a pair of waders and a vest rigged with pockets to hold the small tools of a fly-fisherman's craft. Or in this case, a fly-fisherwoman's craft since the waders and vest appeared to be of a woman's size. The fishing gear rested on some sort of white fabric that was protected by another plastic sheath. The Sheriff took a closer look and then reached in and held it up. It was a wedding dress.

Everyone stared at the items that had been buried in the small coffin, and then at each other, for an uncomfortably long time. Meier's expression seemed to change briefly at the sight of the objects but quickly reverted to surliness.

"Karl," the Sheriff said gently, "you mind telling us why you buried these things?"

Meier didn't reply.

"I know it's probably hard," the Sheriff said as he tried again, "but sometimes it's better to talk about something like this."

Meier finally looked up. Gus could feel the anger as Meier's ferret-like eyes locked briefly on his. "That stuff belonged to my wife," he said in a voice that was barely audible.

"Okay," the Sheriff said, "but why did you bury it?"

"You wouldn't understand," Meier said in the same low voice, looking away again.

"Try me."

After a few moments, Meier began to speak in a halting voice.

"When Alice was kidnapped by that psycho Jemkow and the law stopped looking for them, I couldn't handle it. Me and Alice went fishing every opening day for 18 years. I bought her all of them things." He gestured toward the coffin.

The Sheriff nodded sympathetically. Out of the corner of his eye Gus could see Herb do the same.

"If they'd found her body," Meier continued, "I could have had her laid out proper. Maybe found some closure." He brushed at one eye with the back of his hand. "But they never found nothin', so I just buried the things that remind me of her. Every year on opening day I dig them up and sit with them to remember how things was between us."

When Meier had finished, Gus could feel all eyes trained on him. They were like lasers, dissecting his body's cells. Herb had a "you've really done it this time" expression.

"It's pretty clear we owe you a heartfelt apology, Mr. Meier," the Sheriff said. His eyes were like slits and didn't leave Gus. "For these two men to intrude on your private grief in this way is just inexcusable. We'll get all of this cleaned up for you. If you'd like, I'm sure I could get the county to pay for some sort of marker to commemorate this spot."

As Meier nodded, there was another momentary change in his expression.

Gus continued to stare at the objects in the small coffin. Had he been wrong? He'd sometimes feared that a lifetime of dealing with human nature at its worst had conditioned him to suspect evil in anything that was the least bit unusual. Had that happened here? Maybe, but then his instincts were usually pretty good and something about what he'd just witnessed bothered him. It seemed a little too pat, a little too cute. And that change in Meier's expression. Was it relief from being able to share his grief? Or was it something else? Gus decided he damned sure was going to find out. He grabbed the shovel, jumped into the hole and began to dig.

"What the hell are you doing, Minetti?" the Sheriff screamed, throwing up his hands. "Get out of there!"

Gus dug with a fury, ignoring the Sheriff's commands. Dirt flew as he concentrated on one spot to penetrate down as fast as possible. His chest hurt, like sometimes when he shoveled wet snow, but he kept digging. Herb and the Deputy just stood there, mouths agape, as the Sheriff continued to shout commands and Gus continued to ignore them.

Then Gus's shovel struck something. It wasn't a rock; he knew the sound of a shovel striking a rock. It didn't feel like a root, either. He continued to dig. The object he'd struck was flat, like a board. Maybe the lid of another coffin? Gus continued to scrape, barely hearing the Sheriff's angry voice now. It was a board. He'd been right! That whole scene a few minutes ago had been nothing but a charade!

Gus stood up and looked at the Sheriff, whose face was flushed and looked ready to explode. "I'm coming up, Sheriff, but there's something here you should see."

"Dammit, Minetti, what are you talking about? I'm about to run you in."

"See for yourself. Unless I miss my guess, there's another coffin down there and this one probably doesn't have fishing gear in it."

The Sheriff had the confused expression of a man for whom events had spun out of control. He peered into the hole where Gus stood. "Sam," he finally said after Gus banged the board with his shovel, "get down there and take a look."

Sam's shoulders slumped, but he dutifully exchanged places with Gus in the hole and went to work again. After a little more digging he said, "Sheriff, there's definitely another box down here and this one looks bigger!"

"Damn!" the Sheriff said. He looked at Meier. "What's this all about, Karl?"

Meier's mouth twitched and his eyes darted toward the porch rail where he'd left his shotgun, apparently forgetting that the Sheriff had moved it. The Sheriff, following his eyes, drew his service revolver and moved the shotgun farther out of reach.

"I think I can answer your question, Sheriff," Gus said. "Mr. Meier here found out about his wife carrying on with Marcus Jemkow and killed them both. Then he came up with this cute little gimmick of burying her fishing gear over the real grave as a cover just in case someone became suspicious and started poking around."

The Sheriff looked at Meier for a long time and then back at Gus. "How about Jemkow?" he asked. "Where's he?"

"Can't say for sure," Gus said, "but there's an area at the other end of Meier's property that you might want to check out. You know how the wildflowers are everywhere at this time of the year? That place is mostly barren. Maybe because of the clay that wound up on top when the other grave was dug."

The Sheriff stared at the grave. "Damn," he said again, shaking his head. "Karl, I got to read you your Miranda rights.

Gus noticed Herb staring at him with an astonished expression on his face. He smiled.

THE LAST DEAL

The call troubled Pete Thorsen. It wasn't like Sam Lawrence to phone him in the evening, much less while he was out to dinner with a client.

When Pete got back to Sears & Whitney, he hurried to Sam's office and found him hunched over a small conference table in one corner of his office, staring intently at a thick document. A jumble of paper covered the table, like it had been dumped from a box, and crumpled scraps littered the floor nearby. That wasn't like Sam either. Pete's old friend and mentor was the most meticulous man he knew. Even in his prime, Sam's office had always looked like the set for a magazine shoot rather than the workplace of one of the busiest and most successful lawyers in Chicago.

Something else set off alarm bells in Pete's mind. A revolver large enough to require a manservant to lug it around was lying on Sam's polished mahogany desk.

Sam glanced up when Pete tapped lightly on the door. He looked pale and drawn and Pete suddenly had a sick feeling in the pit of his stomach. It must be a health problem, Pete thought as his eyes wandered toward the revolver again.

Maybe that's what Sam wanted to talk about. But why now, at this time of the night?

"Thanks for coming," Sam said without really looking at him. "I hope I didn't interfere with your client dinner." His tired voice matched his appearance, and when he placed his hands on the table to hoist himself from the chair, it seemed to require an effort.

Pete forced a smile. "No thanks required. Your call actually saved me from sitting around Gibsons all night watching the guy drink and listening to him babble."

It was late in the evening and Sam was still clad in his navy blue, three-piece suit. His trademark gold watch fob, the kind that might have been worn by a banker or prosperous merchant a century earlier, spanned a waistline that was a testament to good food. Looking at him, Pete couldn't help but be conscious of his own open-necked shirt and worn if still serviceable sport coat. Sam hadn't embraced business casual when the firm's partners voted for it six years earlier. In fact, it sometimes seemed as though he'd gone even more formal just to make a point about how he thought a lawyer should dress.

"You okay?" Pete asked. "You look a little peaked."

"Yeah, fine," Sam said softly as he walked across the room. "Can I get you a glass of port?"

Pete arched an eyebrow. "You still have some of the good stuff?"

Sam didn't come back with his usual snappy rejoinder. Instead, he held up a bottle and said, "This 1982 Sandeman's okay?"

Pete grinned and gave a thumbs-up sign. As he watched Sam rummage around for clean glasses, he was conscious, as he had been when he'd returned to the office a few minutes earlier, of how quiet the floor was. There was something eerie about the stillness of a business office late at night that made a person want to step more lightly and speak in hushed tones. Pete chuckled to himself. Maybe he just didn't want to risk stirring up the ghosts of founding partners Nathaniel Sears and John Whitney.

After they'd settled into a pair of wine-colored leather chairs, Pete sat back and waited for Sam to raise what was on his mind. He decided to let him take his time.

"Quiet in here tonight," Pete said, breaking the awkward silence. "Our business must be down. No one but you here, at least on this floor."

Sam sipped his port and stared through the open office door. "The cleaning crew is gone," he said, sounding as distracted as he looked. "They'd finished their work so I let them go early. Sometimes we forget that they have families, too."

Pete bit his lip and nodded. While Sam had retained his spacious corner office, he was now "of counsel" to the firm, a largely honorary title under their structure, and had no client responsibility or authority of any kind. But that didn't prevent him from occasionally exercising the prerogatives he'd once enjoyed when he was the managing partner. Sam also regularly acted as a self-appointed ombudsman for the non-legal staff. The staff, understandably, loved him for it, but his actions annoyed many of the partners.

Pete said nothing about the cleaning crew transgression. Instead, he jerked a thumb in the direction of Sam's desk. "What's the artillery for?"

Sam's eyes flicked toward the desk and lingered on the revolver. His face was impassive and he seemed to search for the right words. "I was cleaning it earlier," he said. "I fired it today."

"Umm," Pete murmured. "Maybe that's what I smelled when I came in."

Except for fly-fishing, Sam's only hobby was collecting Old West memorabilia. He liked to rotate his collection so part of it was always in his office, where he typically still arrived by eight and stayed into the evening. A Civil War-era saddle hung on a mount across the room, under a cavalry saber and a pair of derringers that supposedly had been used by a faro dealer in Deadwood, South Dakota. Pete knew that Sam liked to take some of his old firearms, if they could be safely fired, to a local range from time-to-time.

"What kind of gun is that?" Pete asked.

Sam continued to gaze at the weapon. "It's an original model Colt Frontier Six-Shooter. The dealer who sold it to me claims it was the piece Frank McLaury carried in the gunfight at the O.K. Corral in 1881."

"You believe him?" Pete asked, wondering if Sam had been taken in.

"Hard to know," Sam said, shrugging, "but it's the genuine article. One of the best sidearms ever made."

"You know," Pete said, being something of an Old West aficionado himself, "some people believe the Clantons and McLaurys were innocent victims in that fight."

Sam's expression was even more brooding than when Pete had arrived. "A grand jury did consider whether murder charges should be brought against Wyatt Earp and Doc Holliday," he said, "but they were never indicted. It shows that not everyone who commits an act someone believes is wrong is a murderer."

Pete frowned. "Sam," he said, deciding to bring the conversation to a head, "this is all very interesting, but I doubt you called me just to share a glass of port and talk about the Old West. I have a feeling something is wrong."

Sam stared at his right hand as he slowly flexed it. Arthritis ran in his family and he'd often expressed concern that it would eventually hit him, too. Pete saw no obvious signs of the disease, but the tremble was very noticeable. Maybe he was just feeling the effects of his target practice.

"I wanted to talk to you about Littlefield Industries," Sam said slowly as he continued to work his fingers. "I've been very concerned that a deal we're working on for them is being mishandled."

A red flag snapped up in Pete's mind. The relationship with Littlefield had been nurtured by Sam from the time it was a start-up and the company was now one of the firm's largest clients. Under firm policy, responsibility for overseeing Littlefield's legal business had been transitioned to another partner, Larry Serini, several years earlier when Sam had reached his extended retirement age of 68.

Pete studied Sam's face, which remained as impassive as a sphinx. "How is it being mishandled?"

"A lot of ways," Sam said, not meeting Pete's gaze. "The structure of the deal is bad for Littlefield tax-wise, and we aren't receiving adequate protection against the target company's liabilities."

Pete continued to look at Sam. "How do you know all this? Larry Serini is personally leading our team on that deal, isn't he?"

"He's supposed to be," Sam said softly, still looking away, "but we're not getting the job done. Littlefield isn't receiving the quality of representation they've come to expect from our firm."

Damn it, Sam, Pete thought, *you've got to let go.* They'd been over this in the past, and not just once. The conversation was always the same, like a scene in a bad movie that kept repeating itself. Serini wasn't being responsive to Littlefield's needs. Serini's strategy in a regulatory matter was all wrong. Or, like now, Serini was mishandling some deal.

"Did Larry talk to you about it? Is that how you know all this?"

Sam's eyes were fixed on the documents he'd been studying when Pete came in. "We talked about the deal a couple of weeks ago. I offered to help. He said he'd get back to me, but he never did." He paused. "I think he's afraid to have me around my own client."

Pete continued to press him. "So that's how you know about the structure, from your conversation with Larry."

Sam's eyes were hooded by his bushy white brows. "I saw the drafts," he said slowly. "You'd be shocked at what we've been giving away in that deal."

"I still don't understand," Pete said. "How did you happen to see the drafts? Did Larry give them to you?"

"You're interrogating me, Pete. We should be focusing on how the deal is being mishandled, not this other stuff. Here, let me show you."

Pete followed Sam over to the conference table. The documents covering the table were various drafts of a merger agreement pursuant to which Littlefield would acquire a company named EVtech. The drafts oozed red ink, like a body bleeding from a hundred slashes, and copious notes appeared in the margins. It all appeared to be the result of Sam's sharp pen. A separate chart, again looking like Sam's handiwork, tracked changes to key provisions as negotiations had progressed.

After glancing at the documents, Pete shifted his gaze back to Sam. "You've been avoiding my question," he said, beginning to suspect the worst. "You didn't get all of this from Larry, did you?"

Sam finished making an additional note on one of the drafts and then said, "I really don't see how that's important, but if you must know, I got them from Millie in Word Processing. She's been retyping all of the drafts and became concerned over some of the things she'd seen. She's been with us a long time, as you know, and has the firm's best interests at heart."

Pete grimaced and shook his head. "You shouldn't be going behind Larry's back like this. He's a very competent lawyer and I'm sure there are sound reasons for any concessions he's had to make to get the deal done. Dealmaking is give and take; you know that. And a staff person, no matter how good, just isn't qualified to make judgments on these things."

Sam's lips tightened and his face looked even more ashen. "Not everyone agrees that Serini is a good lawyer," he said. "He was just acceptable to Littlefield because he's a law school friend of the new general counsel." He paused. "Harvey Littlefield isn't impressed with him, I can tell you that. He thinks Serini is a lightweight."

Pete's irritation was bubbling near the surface now. When Pete became the firm's new managing partner, he'd had the unpleasant task of reminding Sam that his three-year grace period from the firm's mandatory age 65 retirement policy was up and Larry Serini would be taking over responsibility for the Littlefield client relationship. In hindsight he realized that no one, himself included, would have been acceptable to Sam as a successor. Sam was unalterably opposed to the retirement policy and it was now clear he believed just as strongly that no one could fill his shoes with Littlefield.

"Sam," Pete said as gently as he could, "Harvey's own board of directors eased him out years ago. He was a great man and did a tremendous job building the company, but everyone knows he's been losing it. At some point, it just becomes time to move on. It will happen to all of us."

Sam's eyes looked even more unfocused and his hands continued to tremble noticeably. Time had overtaken him, Pete thought, as he remembered how it was when he'd begun working for Sam as a young associate. Sam, an imposing figure, would sit in his office surrounded by his team — typically Pete and several specialists — and consider how to deal with some thorny legal issue facing a client. His eyes would twinkle under those massive brows as he solicited input from each of them. Occasionally he would offer some ideas or observations of his own or sum up the collective wisdom of the group. His love for the practice of law was so transparent, so contagious, that everyone would leave the meeting feeling good about themselves and the world. Now Sam looked tired and old. And, Pete feared, possibly suicidal.

"I never wanted to retire," Sam finally said in a tone so soft it was barely audible. "What was I going to do? Marian is gone," he continued, referring to his late wife, "and a man can only do so much fishing."

"Just a minute," Pete said, trying to lighten the mood. "I remember sharing a glass of port with you on another occasion and you told that one of your personal goals in life was to fish every important trout stream in the world. You must have a few to go."

"Things change." Sam continued to stare at the draft he held in his hands, slowly turning the pages. Then he added, again in the same low, weary voice, "I guess I thought I'd get a better shake from you."

The comment jolted Pete. That was bullshit! He'd shown Sam extraordinary deference and in fact had spent a lot of personal political capital within the firm to protect him on numerous occasions.

"That's not fair," Pete said, unable to keep the edge out of his voice. "I manage the firm now, but the partners set the basic policies. You know that. And as I recall, I'm the one who dredged up enough support to get you a three-year extension of the mandatory retirement age."

Sam continued as though he hadn't heard Pete. "I don't know why there's this rush to put people out to pasture these days," he said. "It's a huge waste of human capital. Look at Sir Edward Coke." He pointed toward a bookcase that contained leather-bound volumes of the famed seventeenth century English jurist's work. "He was 76 when he helped author the Petition of Right. That's like being 90 today. Richard Strauss composed until he was 85. Michelangelo designed the dome in St. Peter's when he was 71. I could give you other examples."

"I hear you," Pete replied, "but times have changed. Many firms have gone to an even younger retirement age than ours."

"That doesn't prove anything. It's still a waste, and unfair to people who can still contribute."

Pete decided that nothing would be gained by continuing to debate the policy issue with him. "Have you followed up with Larry?" he asked, realizing he was grasping at straws. "Maybe he just forgot to get back to you."

Sam's expression changed briefly, as though a cloud had passed over his face. "He didn't forget. And yes, I followed up with him twice, including today."

"And?"

"He told me he didn't need my help."

Suddenly Pete felt weary. "What do you want me to do, Sam?"

Sam was staring at one of the drafts again. "Use your authority as managing partner to protect the client's interests," he finally said. The request sounded rehearsed, but his voice was halting and weak, as it had been throughout their conversation. "Put me in charge of finishing the EVtech transaction. It will be my last deal. The firm owes me that."

The entitlement comment made Sam sound like one of the GenXers he liked to rail against. Pete let it pass and said, "Are you serious? I know what you think of him, but Larry Serini seems firmly in control."

"We don't have much time," Sam said, his voice little more than a hoarse whisper. "Littlefield needs me on this one. The firm needs me, too. There isn't anyone else."

Pete furled his brow. "What do you mean? Larry has a full team in place."

"You don't understand, Pete. Before you came over tonight, I had to kill Serini to protect the client."

Some of these stories first appeared elsewhere, but have been significantly modified for this collection. "Cash Affair" was published in *Futures Mystery Anthology Magazine* (March – April 2007). "The Burglar's Tale" was published in *Crime and Suspense* (June 2007). "The Rocks" was published in *Spinetingler Magazine* (Summer 2007). "The Last Deal" was published in *Shred of Evidence* (August 27, 2007). "Opening Day" was published in *Coffee Cramp eZine* (October 2007). And "Dominic's Art" was published in *Mysterical-E* (Fall 2008).

MALICE

ONE

Pete Thorsen couldn't tear his eyes away from the body on the green. The man was naked except for pale blue boxer shorts and his arms and legs were splayed out like the figure in the old Leonardo da Vinci drawing. Blood caked the left side of his face. It had seeped into the turf around his head and left stains that looked black in the early morning light.

"Jesus," muttered Harry McTigue who had struggled up one of the large mounds that ringed the green to join Pete. He was still breathing hard from their trot down the eighteenth fairway of the soon-to-open Mystic Bluffs Golf Club.

Pete heard his friend, but his eyes remained riveted on the grisly scene less than 50 feet in front of him. The man's skin had turned gray, which Pete knew happened when the heart stopped pumping blood through the body, and everything looked surreal. Footprints dotted the dewy ground and yellow crime-scene tape hung lifelessly in the still air. After circling the green, the tape jutted out to seal off a corridor between the mounds that ran out to the golf cart parking area for the hole. Uniformed police officers, most with Sheriff's

Department emblems on their sleeves, milled around outside the tape. They tried to look busy, but mostly just snuck looks at the battered body staked to the green.

"Do you recognize the guy?" Harry asked in a low voice.

Pete shook his head slowly. His eyes were now fixed on the golf club, a middle iron as best he could tell, that lay on the green. He assumed it was the murder weapon since its face was coated with dry blood, and shuddered as he visualized the killer repeatedly striking the victim's head with the club.

Harry stared for a while longer and then looked at Pete again over his half-glasses and as though uncomfortable with the silence, said in the same low voice, "It's a good thing Cap called when he did."

They'd been on their way to the Little Manistee River for a day of trout fishing when Harry's contact, a grizzled veteran of the Sheriff's office named Ernie Capwell, called and told him someone had reported that a body had just been found on the new golf course. He said the whole Department was on their way over. Harry's love of trout fishing was surpassed only by his dedication to ferreting out the news for his weekly, *The Northern Sentinel*, and he told Pete they had to make a detour to Mystic Bluffs. He'd done a sharp u-turn on the highway before Pete could say anything.

Thinking back to how he had no choice in the matter, he just grunted. Yeah, he thought cynically, a real stroke of luck. He'd looked forward to a day of fishing, but instead found himself standing around watching the authorities fuss over the body of a murder victim for the second time in less than a year.

"I see Cap," Harry said. "I'm going to see if he'll talk to me."

Pete watched him make his way down the mound toward where Cap was standing with another Deputy. Harry maneuvered his egg-shaped body through the small crowd of gawkers and looked more squat than ever in his worn tan fishing vest with artificial flies hooked in the fabric and other fishing paraphernalia sticking out of the pockets. Harry had a lot of idiosyncrasies, but none more curious than when he planned to go fishing. Part of his ritual on those days was to put on his fishing vest as soon as he got dressed. He ate breakfast with it on and then would sit in the car on the way to the trout stream looking like an overstuffed mannequin. Pete once asked him why he didn't wait to don his gear when they got to their destination like everyone else. Harry had shot him a sly look and said that wearing the vest helped get him in the "zone" and ready to do battle with the brookies and rainbows and other species that populated the waters of Michigan's prime trout streams. Pete smiled at the thought and rolled his eyes.

As Pete waited for Harry to return, his eyes wandered toward the rocky knob that loomed high over the green and served as the tee area for the par-three hole. He'd played other courses that had holes with similar topography. Balls would float through the air as though suspended by parachutes and, if you had the right club, would slowly descend to the green. With Lake Michigan in full view on one side and rolling, forested terrain on the other, it was the signature hole on a tract that had a lot of them.

A photographer with Sheriff's Department credentials dangling from a chain around her neck had just arrived. Pete recognized her from that day on the beach the previous summer when Cara Lane's body had been found in Clear Lake.

After conferring with the authorities on site, she began to take photos, slowly working her way around the perimeter of the green. She finished the long-distance shots and ducked under the police tape to begin work closer in. When she finished photographing the ground around the body, she zoomed in on the hands and feet of the victim that had been lashed to the stakes by some form of ties. Finally she got to his battered head, and in the silence, he could hear the camera click away. Pete was impressed with her thoroughness and professionalism and knew that her work would be important evidence if the killer were apprehended and the case went to trial.

"You'll never believe who that is," Harry said breathlessly after he'd scrambled back up the mound.

"I'll bet you're going to tell me," Pete said, only half-listening as he continued to watch the photographer.

"Les Brimley."

Pete's head jerked around and he looked at Harry. "You're kidding."

"Nope. It's Brimley. Cap told me they've made the ID."

Pete looked back at the man on the green. Brimley was the man whose firm was developing Mystic Bluffs. It would be, according to him, the premier golf community in northern Michigan. That was saying something in an area which already had Crystal Downs and Arcadia Bluffs and the Bear, among other tracts. Brimley had acquired the property from the estate of James Underhill six years earlier, and the scuttlebutt was that he'd coveted it since shortly after he started coming to the Clear Lake area. That was 10 years ago, not long after Pete bought his own cottage. Following a long battle with the regulatory authorities and various opposition groups, he'd finally prevailed and moved forward with construction. Now he was stretched out dead like a hunting trophy on the signature hole of his own course.

"There's no chance of a mistake?" Pete asked.

"Nope, they're sure."

"Who said it was Brimley?"

"The head pro and another employee," Harry said. "I guess Brimley's wife is on her way over."

Pete thought about that for a while. "If they've already identified the body, why are they subjecting the widow to this spectacle?"

Harry shrugged. "Cap said she became hysterical when they told her. She insisted on coming over. I'm with you, though. This is not something you'd want the spouse to see."

Pete looked thoughtful for a moment. "Did she go home last night?" he asked.

"From what Cap tells me, she stayed with her friend at Glen Lake after the show."

Pete mulled that over. He had been at the show with Harry. It had been a private affair. Private was a bit of a misnomer. Everyone in the area seemed to be there. The woman hosting the event had a low-slung modern house right on the lake. She must have owned several hundred feet of lake frontage that offered an unobstructed view of the water. Pete had a good view from his cottage on the west end of Clear Lake, but in comparison, his place was mere servant's quarters.

Pete was on the invitation list for the show because he owned one of Susan's pieces. He'd bought it in the gallery in town a couple of years earlier and barely knew the artist. In fact, they had met only once and Pete was convinced Susan Brimley didn't know him from the next cottager. Pete knew who she was, though. Susan was a striking woman, with wide-set eyes, an attractive figure, and long dark hair that she was fond of tossing to keep it out of her face. Harry, whom he had dragged along with the promise of dinner at nearby La Becasse that evening, caught him staring at her on more than one occasion and lost no opportunity to remind him that she is a married woman. But Harry's mind was really on the reservation at one of his favorite restaurants in the area and he had dragged Pete out before he had a chance to make his way through the crowd to strike up a conversation with Susan Brimley.

Pete turned back and stared at the green again. The sun was rising in the sky and had begun to burn off the dew and dissolve the footprints left by the Sheriff's Department personnel who were permitted inside the tape. Brimley's body — assuming that's who it was — was still tied to the stakes. The photographer had finished with the green and was now working her way down the path to the golf cart parking area. She was busy taking pictures of the ground.

"This could tear the community apart," Harry said, looking thoughtful.

Pete frowned. "How so?"

"You haven't been around to see this every day like I have," Harry said. "Things have only settled down in the last year or so as the opponents of the development accepted the inevitable. Now people will start picking away at the scabs again and there'll be all sorts of recriminations as supporters of the project worry about whether someone will step into Brimley's shoes and carry things forward. They'll point fingers at the opponents of the project. Stuff like that."

Pete studied Harry for a minute. "Do you think one of them might have killed him?"

"People opposed to the development? Who knows? Things got pretty ugly for a couple of years and Brimley made a lot of enemies. The environmentalists, people who didn't like expansion of the airport, Jim Underhill's heirs who felt Brimley had bought the property for a song. They were all riled up. Then there was that Native American guy."

Pete had paid enough attention to the politics of the Mystic Bluffs development to know they were standing on ground that was one of the reasons the project was so contentious. For decades, long before Underhill acquired the property, the area had been the site of annual Native American pow wows, the meeting place of the so-called "Three Fires" of the Ojibwa, Ottawa, and Odawa tribes. The rocky knob that the course architect selected to be the tee area for the seventeenth hole held special meaning for them. A nineteenth century Ojibwa chief had had his vision on "The Rock," as the knob came to be known. Legend had it that on his fourth day in the wilderness, fasting as he was required to do, a wolf appeared before the youth as he sat on The Rock. The wolf spoke to him and came back each of the following two days and counseled him on how to deal with the European settlers who were increasingly encroaching on tribal lands. The vision became the chief's roadmap for the pacts he sought to craft with the white man. A descendent of the chief, a man named Leonard Talks With Wolves who'd taken his ancestor's name, fought against the development along with the environmentalists, but mostly he opposed including The Rock in the golf course layout. In the end, the lure of designing a memorable hole was too much for Brimley and his architect to resist and they not only included The Rock but made seventeen the signature hole and included pictures of it in all their marketing materials. Thinking they were honoring the chief, they then rubbed salt in the wounds of Talking Wolf and his followers by naming the development Mystic Bluffs.

"I know about the environmentalists and the Native American groups, but Brimley had a lot of supporters, too, didn't he?" Pete asked.

"He did. Most of the town people supported him. They smelled jobs and economic development. The county fathers were salivating over the higher tax base that would come with the development. This is a damn poor area, you know."

Pete turned back to the photographer who was still taking pictures of the path. "The course was supposed to open in a week or two, if I remember," he said.

"June 11. I understand that only 14 lots have been sold, though. The economy and all that bullshit. Brimley had to make the course semi-private, at least temporarily, and cut the greens fees to draw people in. There have been a lot of rumors about the project being in financial trouble."

Pete nodded and continued to watch the photographer.

After a few more minutes, Harry continued and said, "I wonder why the killer dragged Brimley way out here to beat his brains in. He risked someone seeing him, didn't he?"

Pete shrugged. "You'd think so."

"Any theories?" asked Harry, studying Pete carefully and prodding him to get involved in his speculation.

Pete thought about the last time he'd become obsessed with a crime and how he'd let it take over his life. That was less than a year earlier, and when it was all over, he'd promised himself he wasn't going to let it happen again. He had responsibilities to his stepdaughter, Julie, and the experience had already caused him to reevaluate his life and step aside as managing partner of his law firm. The last thing he needed, or wanted, was to put himself in that kind of spot again.

Pete just shrugged.

"You have no theories or you have none you're willing to talk about?" Harry asked as he continued to study him.

"Both."

Harry wasn't one to give up easily. "For a guy to kill another man by beating him to death with a golf club, there had to be a lot of passion behind it. And then like I said, to drag him way out here, it's almost like he was sending a message."

Pete had thought of the same thing. And Harry was right, the killer was taking a chance when he dragged Brimley's body out to the golf course to kill him. There could be a reason for it. But this wasn't his fight. He was perfectly content to let acting Sheriff Franklin Richter handle it. That was his job, regardless of what Pete thought of him.

As the morning wore on, the crowd of onlookers grew in size and two more people — they looked like crime scene investigators — joined the Sheriff's Department personnel and were scouring the crime scene for evidence. Another man carrying a large shoulder bag walked up and conferred with Richter.

"Who's the guy in the striped shirt?" Pete asked.

Harry squinted in his direction. "I think that's the Medical Examiner's assistant," Harry replied. "I'm a little surprised that Ethan isn't here himself."

After five minutes of conversation with Richter, the man ducked under the tape, conferred with the crime scene team, and then knelt and studied the body. Pete shifted his gaze to the two technicians. They were examining something on the ground. They looked at a patch of ground, then moved farther up the path and examined another patch of ground.

After conferring a second time, they beckoned the photographer over and had her take more pictures. From 50 feet away, the area looked just like the surrounding ground, but obviously they'd spotted something. Richter walked over to join them, taking care to stay close to the tape. He squatted down and let his eyes follow where the technicians pointed, then moved forward and did the same thing. He spoke to the technicians in a low voice. Pete couldn't hear what they were saying, but assumed they were discussing whatever it was that they'd found.

Richter finally stood and hitched up his pants. He glanced up at the onlookers on the mounds surrounding the green, and when he saw Pete, he locked eyes with him and stared.

ABOUT THE AUTHOR

Robert Wangard splits his time between Chicago, where he practiced law, and northern Michigan. His first novel, *Target*, a Pete Thorsen Mystery, was published in April 2010. He is a member of Mystery Writers of America, the Short Mystery Fiction Society, and other writers' organizations.